Believe In Love

Claudia Loens

DEDICATION

To three of my best friends…Tami Wiedensmith,
Karen Adamski and Ann-Marie Abbott. You ladies
inspired me the most when I was single. You loved and
encouraged me every step of the way. And always,
always, you taught me to believe in love.

ACKNOWLEDGMENTS

The cover of this book was a painting that one of my best friends, Karen Adamski, painted for me specifically for this book. She has always encouraged my writing and has been one of my biggest fans. Having her artwork on the cover of this book is like a kiss of good luck. Thank you, Karen!

My husband continues to support and inspire my dreams. He made me believe in love again. My daughters are always ready to cheer me on and they are the wind behind me.

A special thank you to my parents, Jim and Marlene Courselle. They've ALWAYS believed in me and and were generous with their praise and love. I could only hope to be as good of a parent to my girls, as they were for me. I love you, Mom and Dad.

Prologue

The scraggly teenager lumbered past the security guard, insolently looking both irritated and bored as he was told to stand on the line while the guard swiped the metal detector wand over his person. Another guard searched through the worn duffle bag until he came to the item in question.

"It's just a diving watch," the guard told his co-worker.

"Move along," the other guard said, already focused on the next passenger.

With a rude snap of his gum, the kid grabbed at the bag and proceeded to the gate where his flight would leave in a half hour. *Just a diving watch*, he snickered. *That's what they thought.*

1

Molly Carson sat at the bar, sipping her blue Hawaiian drink and gazing at the ocean, not more than fifty yards away. Ahhh. This is the life, she thought. Despite the fact that she was here because of her sense of duty, Molly vowed to herself that she would make the most of this tropical getaway. Roger had told her that the break would do her good, and as usual, with the thought of Roger – handsome, charismatic, Roger- a lump of emotion clogged her throat. It was all too new, too fresh to be anything except an open wound.

"Would you like another drink, Miss?" The native bartender looked at her as he wiped down the bar. He noticed the sadness in her pale blue eyes and shook his head.

A woman so young and beautiful should not have such sadness. It wrenched at his old heart. She wasn't the first to come to Kauai to heal, though he was almost certain it was her first time on the island.

She did not have the look of a well-travelled woman. In fact, she looked like she was more comfortable in her own familiar surroundings. When she didn't respond, he prodded gently, "Miss?"

Startled by the offer - because she'd almost forgotten that she was drinking alcohol, Molly nodded. She had read a lot about Kauai and knew that the locals were very friendly. Nonchalantly, she glanced down at her large straw purse where a copy of *Travel Magazine* (one of her few secret vices) was safely tucked. "Thank you," she said politely as the bartender put the blue drink in front of her. At this rate she'd be smashed by dinner, she thought.

"This your first time in Kauai?" He was being friendly again, though Molly wasn't here for the company. It felt foreign to her to make small talk with strangers. She was used to the solitude of her own thoughts. With resolve, she tossed her wavy brown hair over her shoulder and looked him in the eye. She needed the practice. "Yes."

"Well, Aloha, then."

His friendliness was contagious. She raised her drink to him and returned the greeting with a warm smile, "Aloha!"

That's how he saw her when he walked onto the sandy deck of the outdoor bar. She was quite out of place – so obviously a tourist that he had to smile. She had a big straw hat sitting on the bar next to her big, bulky straw purse. She wore a crisp new sundress and sandals that looked like they were causing her winter feet to blister and she sat up straight as a pin. Her skin was as pale as the white sand, her eyes bluer than the ocean. Her smile, though shared with half a heart, was a bit crooked.

He pegged her as a Librarian and certainly not his usual type, but he was amused enough by the smile. He felt the gentle nudge of his body's response to her as he took the stool next to her. He'd just enjoy the company.

Bristling when the huge man sat beside her, Molly quickly moved her hat out of his way. "Thank you," he said in a voice she thought was appropriately deep for his enormous size. She nodded in acknowledgement. Why did he have to sit beside her? There were at least a dozen empty stools around the bar - perhaps she should move to one of them? But then again, that would be terribly rude. And Molly Carson was NEVER rude. Sighing, she sipped at her drink, which tasted better with every sip.

She never went to bars. Well, that wasn't entirely true. Occasionally a few women from St. Mary's went out for a drink and Roger always urged her to go. But other than a smoky cabernet with a grilled steak, the taste of alcohol did not appeal to Molly.

Bars intimidated her anyway…so full of lusty, cocky men who always felt the need to approach her and offer themselves as part of the menu. Sometimes feigning boredom worked to deter them, but when it didn't, her answer was always the same – no, thank you.

She didn't understand why they approached her in the first place, when her other friends were so beautiful and were more interested in their attentions. Roger used to tell her that she was more beautiful than all of them, but then again, he was biased. A smile crossed her face at the memory and then quickly faded as she recalled the recent turn of events. She stared sadly into the depths of the blue drink, past the chunk of pineapple perched on the edge of the glass. Her shoulders ever so slightly drooped.

"Carson," said the huge man sitting beside her, holding out his hand in greeting.

Startled, her palm fled quickly to her chest as if in protection and she almost fall off the tottering bar stool. "Excuse me?"

"Carson – my name's Carson," he wasn't the least bit annoyed by her guarded response. Librarians were not known for their friendliness. He figured she was from somewhere in the Midwest too.

The coincidence of his name and hers made her smile and relax somewhat. "I'm Molly. Molly *Carson*." He too understood the joke and returned the smile to her as he shook her hand for a few seconds longer than was necessary. His touch was warm and rough and dry – all pleasing to her delicate hands. She had to tug gently to retrieve her hand and consciously refrained from wiping his vibrant masculine energy off of her hand when he released her.

His presence was distracting her from her thoughtful wanderings, as she was sure he was accustomed to.

"Where are you from?" He asked as the bartender handed him a Corona.

"San Francisco." She didn't mean for her answer to be so curt, but seeing the bartender try to hide a smile, she reminded herself to be more polite. "And you?" Practice, Molly, practice.

"I'm from all over, really. I have a home here in Kauai and in San Francisco, Dallas and New York."

Interested despite her senses telling her to mind her own business, Molly asked, "Why?"

He looked her directly in the eye for the first time, delighting her with unusual deep green eyes flecked with gold. "Because I like it that way." He said it as if the topic were off limits.

Nosiness came naturally with an abundance of curiosity. Always did her in.

"Sorry," she mumbled, looking at her hands. She looked up, her head cocked when she heard him chuckle.

"For what? That I like to live all over or that you wanted to know?"

"Both, I guess." She didn't know what to say. He was much too masculine, much too arrogant – at least she thought he was arrogant – for her taste. She wasn't used to men like this. Despite his rugged handsomeness, she preferred a more refined, gentleman. Like Roger. The memory sent her shoulders drooping uncharacteristically.

Carson watched the emotions play over her face. He imagined that she thought she was guarded and uneasy to read, but she was wrong. He could see – even Sam could see! - that she was dealing with some sort of inner struggle.

Made for easy pickings for him if he was so inclined. It wasn't uncommon for people to come to the islands to heal from something or another. He wondered what her story was and then reminded himself that he didn't need to get involved in someone else's problems.

Especially some clingy female.

Still, the words were out of his mouth before he could stop them. "So what's gotten you crying in your drink, Molly Carson?"

Annoyed and instantly defensive, Molly retorted, "I don't know what you mean."

"I mean that you look sad. You're not supposed to be sad on vacation." He didn't want her to run away while he was still intrigued by her. "Man problems?"

She stared into the depths of the blue drink for a long moment. The tears that were so close to the surface these days threatened to make an appearance and she took a moment to compose herself. "Not exactly."

"Sometimes it helps to talk to a stranger," his voice caressed her like silk sheets on a cold night as he leaned into her, establishing his presence inside her personal space.

"Not for me. I mean – er - thank you, but no. I'm fine." Recovered, she looked up and found his face inches away from hers, his gaze deep and intense.

His face had character…a deep, dark tan and laugh lines around his eyes and mouth which told her he was probably quick to good humor. There was a tiny scar on his forehead, just next to his eyebrow, which had her wondering what had caused it. And those eyes – so sparkly and kind on the surface, but looking deeper sent a silent shudder through Molly.
This man was not what he appeared. Oh, good Lord, he was handsome. She willed herself not to look away and prayed she would be able to breathe again soon.

"Suit yourself, then." He pulled back into his own space on the bar stool, completely aware of her discomfort.

He took a long drink of his beer and she watched – oh how she watched, as his throat worked to take it all in. It was fascinating, really, and she felt herself grow hot just observing it. She had to look away, but not before she noticed a cocky grin on Carson's face.

She was certainly a prickly one, he thought. But how a woman living in liberal San Francisco could end up being a prude, was beyond him. "Have you lived in SF all your life?" He found himself asking.

"No. I was born and raised on a farm in Idaho. Not too far from Boise."

Well that explained it. He smiled, amused. "How'd you get to The City?"

She noticed that he had none of her reluctance whatsoever in asking questions, so she shrugged. "I was young and rebellious and wanted to get out of Idaho. So after college I accepted a job as a nurse at St. Mary's."

Carson had to hold himself back from the guffaw that clawed at his throat. What he had here, was a backwoods, old-fashioned nurse. He hadn't been too far off in his assessment. He could certainly see her in her white nurse's outfit; hair tucked tighter than a baseball and white squeaky rubber shoes as she took some old geezer's blood pressure. It did something strange to him and he felt his loins leap at the vision. Humph. Who knew he had a secret nurse fantasy in his horny head?

Not certain what had caused that smirk on his face, Molly suddenly felt uneasy. She prayed to be sucked up by the sand at her feet, but knew that was too much to wish for. So she diverted his attention away from her, something she was quite adept at. "And you? Where were you born and raised?"

Suddenly serious, Carson stared into his beer for a moment. She thought he might not answer, the time drew out so long. When he finally spoke, his words were abrupt. "Born in Austin, Texas. Raised in a handful of states around the country."

It didn't take a genius to see that he had had an unhappy childhood. Perhaps *he* was the one who needed someone to talk to. Her nurturing instincts kicked in – or perhaps it was the second Blue Hawaiian, but she laid a sympathetic hand on his dark, hairy arm.

"I'm sorry," she said for the second time in fifteen minutes, which had him raising a dark brow in amusement.

"What are you sorry for now, Molly?" He stared at her carefully manicured hand for a moment before, he slowly laid his free hand on top of hers to keep her there. He liked the feel of her gentle touch on his hairy arm, even if she did flinch a little bit at the contact. It had been a while since he'd felt the gentle touch of a woman.

"I – well." A frown creased her perfect brow. She didn't really know how to say this to this handsome stranger and felt certain that anything she said would be insulting. The feel of his cool hand on top of hers was beginning to make her head spin. She was not used to such testosterone. Clearing her throat, she forged ahead, bravely. "I'm sorry you had such a – a difficult childhood." There. She'd said it and he didn't look the least bit angry.

Carson had good instincts too, and his told him to milk the sympathy route and he just might get to fulfill that nurse's fantasy he didn't know he had. "Wellllll," he drawled out, taking advantage of the ten years he'd spent in the south. "I suppose it was no picnic. But I survived."

So engrossed in the beginning of his story, Molly didn't even realize she'd put another hand on top of his and was leaning into his long arm resting on the bar. "Tell me about it," she breathed; now fully feeling the affects of the tropical drink.

"Well, now let's see. I went to kindergarten in

Dallas, third grade in Arkansas, fifth grade in Alabama, seventh grade in Boston, ninth in Montana and graduated high school in Los Angeles." Acutely aware that she was now stroking his arm, he continued. "I went to college in Southern California and eventually took a job in San Francisco."

"It must have been frightening for you as a child," she was giving him her most sympathetic look and now her breast was actually touching his upper arm.

He nodded soberly.

"Why did your family move so often?"

"My father was a salesman and he went wherever the job sent him. He sold hotel supplies. He's retired in Florida now."

She allowed him the thoughtful pause and before he got too lost in his thoughts, she prompted him again. "And your mother?"

"Mom died when I was twelve." This was getting a little too personal for him, nurse-fantasy or not. She seemed to have a way of worming her way into his head and he had to put a stop to it now, before his second beer.

"Oh - I'm so sorry!" She looked stricken, as if it had just happened yesterday and he was reminded of her earlier look of grief. That was it. Now he could name it. She looked grief-stricken.

"Aw, it's ok. We managed."

"How many brothers and sisters do you have?" She wanted to know more and promptly ignored her subconscious telling her that she was practically sitting in his lap and she must mind her manners!

"I'm the oldest of four. Two sisters and a brother."

"And you were twelve when your mother died?!" She made it sound like the most horrific thing on the planet. "You must have had to be very responsible – taking care of your siblings and all."

She was right. He naturally assumed the role his mother had vacated, preparing meals, washing clothes and shopping for his younger brother and sisters. Until his father married that witch of a woman, Eunice. But he was already sixteen by that time and had the independence of a first job and a car...until they moved again. He shuddered visibly at the thought of his crazy stepmother.

Feeling his pain, Molly pulled her hand away and ran it affectionately over his head and back, much the way she would console one of her child patients. Carson felt her ample breast against his arm as she tried to sooth him like a startled colt. He heard the discreet clearing throat from behind the bar, a reminder that it was time to redirect Miss Molly away from the personal details of his life.

"Have dinner with me Molly Carson." His gentle demand was low and gruff and had the slightest drawl to it. He figured he had milked the sympathy routine long enough to have her primed.

As if she suddenly realized where she was and what she was doing, Molly snapped to attention, removed her hand and sat up straight as a pin. She blamed the Blue Hawaiian – oh my, was that her third sitting there on the bar? – It too was empty! She had no business practically laying herself all over this strange, albeit handsome, man! Horrified at her behavior, she attempted to stand.

"I'm sorry, but I can not." She made eye contact with the bartender who came over as she fumbled with the contents of the large purse. "Can you please charge this to my room, Sam?" She asked, swaying ever so slightly back and forth.

"Which room is that, miss?"

"Five-zero-six-two," she managed without too much embarrassment. "It was a pleasure to meet you, Carson. Good-bye."

She turned too abruptly and smacked into the barstool and nearly lost her footing. He was up in a second, towering over her at over six feet. He gripped her arm and took her straw hat from the bar.

"Put our drinks on my tab, Sam," Carson said, winking at his friend. "I think you need some assistance back to your room," he said, guiding her toward the lobby elevators.

She thought about fighting him – really she did. He was a stranger and he was just looking for a way to get her back to her room. But common sense won, because she really did need his help. She would deal with him at the door if necessary.

Molly Carson couldn't have been over five foot three, Carson figured. She was petite and slight, but he could feel her strength as she held firmly to his side. Her hair was in her face now – it was everywhere, really, and he resisted the urge to just pick her up and carry her to her room. He did have to remain somewhat professional in this hotel, since it was one that he owned; so he took the difficult path and simply helped her move one step at a time.

She mumbled something about it being shameful that she was drinking at four o'clock in the afternoon and he didn't have the heart to tell her it was already past six. It was quite clear that she was not used to imbibing and he felt a little twang of guilt over his assistance in that area. He almost laughed out loud at her filthy vocabulary, which consisted of a stream of words such as "darn" and "blasted" and "fricken".

On the elevator, she was startled when it moved, jerking her weakened body and she fell into his arms, her breasts pressed firmly into his strong chest. She flipped her hair back and looked up at him, aware of the contact their bodies just made. With lips slightly parted in surprise, it was all Carson could do not to kiss her wholly at that very moment. Luckily for both of them the ride was short and soon they were at her door.

"Key?" he asked politely, thinking that the sooner they parted company, the better. He was not interested in fighting off a drunk woman tonight.

"Key?" She looked at him, somewhat confused before it donned on her. "OH! The key. My key. Of course. Hmmmm." She dug into her purse and pulled out one thing after another and handed them to Carson. Brush. Make-up bag. Tampon. Chapstick. Sunglasses. Wallet.

"No wait," she said taking her wallet back. "I think it's in here."

Successfully, the key fit into the door and electronically released the lock. She pushed it open and stumble-ran into the room, barely landing backwards on the king-size bed, her dress tossed up to her crotch. "Weeeeeee," she said upon landing, further proof that Carson needed to get out of there immediately. The woman was smashed.

He tried to hold out her personal belongings to her, but she took that moment to turn over onto her knees and crawl, seductively (though he didn't think she did it on purpose) up to the top of the bed.

"I – er – I'll put your things here," he motioned

to the bureau, where he knew for certain that her clothes were already neatly unpacked and placed in it's hefty drawers.

"Are you ok then?" He was nervous suddenly and felt that he could not be trusted to stay in her company for very much longer.

"My nightie," she slurred. He winced at the idea of some slinky piece of nothing, but went searching for it nonetheless. He felt a huge wave of relief when he found it neatly folded in the top drawer. Not a silky piece of material after all, but a practical gown of white cotton. On second thought, the image of her in the cotton aroused him much the way the nurse thing did, and he decided he'd had enough.

He practically threw it at her and said shortly, "here you go. I'm leaving now so you can put it on. Good night."

With that he was quickly out the door and leaning against the wall in the hallway. He let out a long breath. What in the hell had just happened? After regaining his composure, he headed back to the bar where he knew Sam was having a good chuckle at his expense.

2

Two things proved to Molly that she was alive when she woke up the following morning. One, she had the worst headache she'd ever experienced in her twenty seven years and, two, her stomach was both growling and rolling at the same time. She was hungry and well, she guessed, hungover. It had never happened to her before, though there was that New Year's Eve with Roger when she had two glasses of champagne. That had given her a headache, but he assured her that everyone got a headache from champagne. *Roger.*

The memories came flooding back. The months spent at his bedside as his personal nurse...the many games of gin rummy in which he never allowed her to win...and finally, that last jaunt to the hospital two weeks before. For weeks she had begged him to let her get him to the hospital, but he wouldn't think of it.

"I want my own bed," he argued, though as the hours passed, his protests became weaker until finally, she simply called the ambulance. But it was too late. He died in her arms five hours later. Sometimes, when she was feeling especially self-deprecating, she wondered if she had called the ambulance sooner, would he have lived? But as a medical professional, she knew she couldn't take the blame.

It was that maddening, incurable disease that took him, not the lack of proper medical care.

And now here she was. In Kauai at his request, sleeping off a hangover. She could just see him, up in heaven having a good chuckle over that one.

A glance at the clock told her that she'd been asleep for more than twelve hours. It was after eight in the morning and she was still in bed. That was so unlike her – especially since the time difference meant it was really ten o'clock at home!

The idea of food both revolted and summoned her. But first things first, she must assess the damage and to do that, she had to actually sit up.

The room shifted when she sat up and then turned completely when she moved her feet over the side of the big bed too quickly. Holding both sides of her face, Molly let herself rest after the brief exertion. She didn't want to open her eyes again, but her will outweighed her self-indulgence. She continued to hold her head as she scooted her bottom toward the edge and eased onto her feet. With one hand on the bed for support and one on her head, she steadied herself.

Poking one eye open, she scanned the room to see if it was still moving. It was. With a deep breath and muttered words of encouragement, she left the safety of the side of the bed with two very brave steps. On the third step, however, she bent over and clutched both her tummy and her head in agony. The bathroom was still a good ten steps away and she was certain she was going to lose the limited contents of her stomach before she made it to the toilet.

Several minutes passed before she felt strong enough to continue her journey.

She gulped in huge mouthfuls of air, which seemed to help her regain some courage.

Each step was a personal challenge as she gained strength with each success. At last, she was leaning against the marble sink, her hair dangling tangled into its bottom. She did it!

When she was finally able to peer into the mirror, she was surprised at how good she looked compared to how she felt. Yes, she was pale and her eyes were red, but overall, she looked…well, she looked hungover. She even managed a gruff chuckle at the idea that Roger would have been howling at her if he'd been there.

Several handfuls of cold water made a vast improvement on her disposition and taking a few gulps of water from the faucet directly into her mouth eased the dryness in her throat. She was ready for phase two - the shower. However brief it was, it went a long way towards making Molly feel human again.

Having slipped her nightgown back over her wet head, Molly was attempting to detangle her hair when a brisk knock sounded at her door. She must have forgotten to put the "please do not disturb" sign on the handle the night before.

"Just a moment, please," she muttered and made her way slowly to the door, still partially bent over in discomfort. With an apologetic half smile on her face, she opened the door, prepared to send the housekeepers away. But it was not the housekeepers that greeted her.

It was a man – yes, the man from last night –

and he was pushing a metal dining cart past her into her room.

"Hello?" She questioned as he moved efficiently, setting the table and pouring her a steaming cup of coffee.

He didn't seem bothered by her haughty tone when she said, "excuse me?! What are you doing?!"

He whisked the metal cover off of the plate and paraded it in front of her nose. "Bacon and eggs and greasy hash browns...hangover food!" He exclaimed proudly and then felt immediate regret when Molly ran to the bathroom and vomited.

"Aw, honey, I'm sorry. I should have asked how you are feeling first."

Ignoring him, she ran the toothbrush through her mouth quickly to get rid of the taste and then whirled – if one could call it a whirl – around to confront him. She didn't give herself a chance to realize that she was beginning to feel better.

"I'm feeling horrible, thank you very much! Who do you think you are waltzing in here with food, assuming that I want any?! And don't call me honey!" The last was said with a shout and an abrupt wave of the hand for extra emphasis.

She looked beautiful as she stood with wet hair in a see-through nightgown that clung to her moist body. His gaze was caught at the wet pucker made by her dark nipples and he had to drag his eyes back to her green face, which was turning pink with anger and now embarrassment as the moments slipped by. Her blue eyes were no longer hazy with hangover, but sharp with acute indignation. She was magnificent.

"Wait a minute," she said, realization slowly dawning on her. "How did you get this tray of food?

And did we…"

Her eyes grew wide in horror as her gaze flew to the bed, a prim hand covering her open mouth. "Did we…DID WE…??" She didn't even know what words to use – it was too ghastly a thought!

"No, we didn't," he sounded disappointed and a little miffed that she would suggest such a thing. "Yet," he added, hoping to see her flare up again. "And as for the tray, I have connections here at the hotel." He decided to leave it at that for now.

"Yet? What do you mean, yet?" She could have cut out her tongue, but by golly she wanted this man to be attracted to her. It must be the remains of the alcohol, but he looked scrumptious standing there in a dark green polo shirt and white shorts that accentuated his tan, muscular body.

He came closer to her then, but only trusted himself enough to stand a foot away. He reached out and grabbed a strand of wet hair and held it up to his nose for a long inhale. "I meant exactly what I said." He looked her directly into her eyes. "We didn't sleep together. Yet."

She had to swallow the look of pure desire that she knew was evident on her face and to do that, she had to look away. Feigning incense, she brushed past him, into the larger part of the room. "You're pretty confident, don't you think?"

He let her have her little temper, though he could see it was at her own expense. He was laughing in his eyes and it piqued her even more. With a huff, she sat on the bed, and then, as if realizing that would only seem like an invitation to him, flew from the bed as if it had burned her bottom and landed in the one straight back chair in the room. He laughed out loud then, thoroughly enjoying her outrage.

At last, he put her out of her misery. "Look, I just thought you could use a hearty breakfast to help you get over the Blue Hawaiians. No obligation. No expectations. Really."

Finally looking at him, she said quietly, "thank you."

"You're welcome." He turned toward the door and she had to fight the wave of disappointment.

"Where are you going?" She found herself asking.

"To work. I have a couple of meetings today. Just make yourself comfortable. I'll find you," he said the last with a grin before closing the door.

"Wait –" She cried and since he didn't hear her, she mumbled to herself, "what's your name?" She felt she should know it, but she couldn't recall it. Shrugging, she set about trying to eat the dreadful breakfast before her.

Carson had a meeting with the head chef, the Hotel Manager and the head of the housekeeping staff. Everything was running smoothly, but in his experience, he needed to check in with everyone to make them feel appreciated. He reviewed all the quarterly reports from each area and the projections from the reservations list. Business was good.

The following day he had an appointment up the coast with a building contractor, who would be reviewing his designs for a movie star's mansion. Architecture was his first passion, but running his hotels was a close second, he thought as he sipped his coffee between meetings.

He felt pride in knowing that he'd designed

every last inch of the hotels under his signature name, Waverly. They were five star quality in both service and grounds.

Carson wondered how a young nurse from San Francisco could afford the price of this elite hotel that usually housed movie stars and rich notables. Maybe she saved her money. Or maybe she lived on credit. Either way, it didn't matter to him as long as the bill was paid.

There was something that intrigued him, something that had his usually focused mind wandering to thoughts of Molly Carson. She was definitely different than Terrie or Nancy or Melissa – his more recent dalliances. Each of them was a glamorous woman with a super-model body, with careers and their own money, though they didn't pretend they didn't like his. They could all go from the golf course to a formal cocktail party, but there was a lack of interest on Carson's part where they were concerned. They were too much alike. Too much his "type", which had gotten boring in the past few years.

And there was the issue that surfaced with every relationship. The "c" word. Commitment. All women eventually wanted it from him, even though he told them from the outset that he was not looking for a commitment. But they all thought they were different, that they could change him. He felt regret when he had to end it at some point when the pressure became too much. He liked his life exactly as it was.

And now he's met Molly. A nurse from Idaho, for crying out loud. She was sexy in her own way, though compared to his other women, she would certainly be considered dowdy.

She intrigued him - it was as simple as that.

And he looked forward to wiping the look of grief from her eyes and replacing it with a look of passion. His work suffered for most of the morning as thoughts of Molly kept playing in his head. Seeing her in the clingy, wet nightgown had his body reacting with an urgency that he hadn't known for a long time.

Despite the voice of warning in his head telling him not to hurt her, he regretted that it couldn't be helped. A woman like that was born to have a home, a husband and babies – nothing he was prepared to offer. Yet her allure was too strong to resist and seldom did he resist allure. So the impending guilt was assuaged with the notion that he would have her, but he would make it an experience she would never forget.

A knock at his door caused him to draw his blurry gaze from the sheets of numbers in front of him. He was ready for a distraction, and he also needed to stretch his long, athletic legs. Despite the fact that his chosen careers caused him to sit at long periods of time, his body was not accustomed to it and rebelled with tightening muscles in his neck and shoulders.

"Come in." His frown turned into a warm smile as his Amenities Director, Leilani, poked her head in, followed by her tall, graceful body. She was an exquisite island beauty with a list of admirers nearly as long as the dark black hair that cascaded down her back to just above her bottom. She didn't hide her adoration of Carson when they were alone, though he thought he'd made it clear that nothing would ever be reciprocated. Not only was she his employee, but she was young – only 22 – and the daughter of his head Concierge and friend, Gus.

Besides, despite her physical beauty, he was not attracted to her in any way other than a brotherly and fatherly way. He'd known her since she was still in high school and regardless of her many adult accomplishments under his management, he still thought of her in a rather juvenile capacity.

"Hello, Carson," her whole body seemed to breathe an air of grace and sensuality as she glided across the room and took the offered seat across from her boss. Carson was reminded that she had won the title of Miss Hawaii several years ago and still presented herself as if she held a carefully perched crown upon her head.

"Hello, Leilani," he stood and paced the room several times, shrugging his shoulders and swinging his arms to get the tension out.

"You need to let me give you a massage," she said as her eyes followed him around the room. Her first position with the Waverly Hotel had been a summer job as his most popular massage therapist during her college years. Upon graduation with a degree in Hospitality Management, she was awarded the position of Spa Supervisor. But during the year since, she had whipped the Spa into one of the most popular features of the hotel and still found time to assist in other areas as well; catering, event planning and kid's camp. At her one year review, Carson created a new position for her, Amenities Director, and gave her a free hand at improving the guest offerings.

"And take you away from our guests? I don't think that would be a very wise business decision." He smiled fondly at her, adeptly side-stepping her offer. She draped her arm over the back of the plush chair, pressing her voluptuous chest against the binds of the V-neck sundress. "Maybe we could schedule it during off hours."

He ignored her comment and the way she carefully displayed herself on his behalf and launched into the business at hand. "I assume you've seen the article?"

Recognizing his determination to conduct business, Leilani opened her portfolio and extracted a copy of the article and dangled it proudly by the corner. "I have it right here!"

"To be written up as one of the top five hotels on the islands was quite a coo last year…but to now be considered one of the top five hotels in the nation from the leading travel magazine…well, I think a large part of the congratulations goes to you, Lei. You've done an outstanding job."

Leilani nodded her head humbly in response to his praise, her long eyelashes batting a slow rhythm against her cheek. "Thank you for listening to my ideas, Carson. I love my job and I love this hotel. I want to make you proud of me."

Carson sat back down behind his desk and took something from the top drawer. "I'm extremely proud of you, Lei. And in appreciation of all of your hard work, I would like you to have this bonus."

"Thank you." She reached across his desk to take the envelope from him, her movement just low enough for him to get a generous view of her cleavage. Coughing, he looked away.

"Aren't you going to open it?" Carson tried to hide his smile. This was one of his favorite duties – employee recognition. When she hesitated, he waved a hand animatedly at her and gave up his serious pretense. "Open it!"

In a rare display of girlishness, she giggled and tore at the envelope. When she withdrew the check, she sat back in her chair with a thump, her mouth hanging open indelicately.

"I – I can't accept this, Carson!"

He laughed at her response, a deep rumble that bled out into the outer offices. "Of course you can. You earned it."

"But it's a third of my salary for a whole year. It's too much!" Her eyes were wide with wonder and awe.

Carson stood again and came around his massive desk to perch himself on the corner in front of her. The old desk groaned with the weight of his substantial form. In all sincerity, he said softly to her, "take it. You worked hard for it and I'm pleased with the results. Consider it incentive to continue doing magical things for my hotel. I'm sure you can think of a way to spend it?"

Nodding excitedly, she brainstormed, "I could pay off my student loans…or buy a new car…or move into a better apartment."

The joy of seeing her delight made Carson chuckle again. She jumped up and threw herself into his arms, reminiscent of her teenage years when she would express her emotions the moment they occurred. "Thank you, thank you!"

He hugged her back and gently pushed her away when the hug lingered too long. She accepted his dismissal with good nature, even though she thought she saw a sparkle of attraction in his eyes. It was something.

"Now," he moved back to his chair and turned the computer monitor sideways so they could both view it. "Let's discuss the quarterly reports you sent me."

Tomorrow. The thought drifted through Molly's sun-drenched, hungover head, as she lay sprawled on the cushy lounge chair on the quiet cement deck, where a lush fountain of dolphins sprayed a cadence of water into the lavish pool. Tomorrow she would do what she needed to do and then she could schedule her trip home. She'd left it open-ended, since she hadn't been certain how long her little mission would take her.

The mission itself was simple, but the nerves she had to drum up to do it, was another thing altogether. She didn't want to think about leaving this beautiful place just yet, but she had a life, pathetic as it may now be, to get back to and things that had to be done.

Maybe she'd plan a trip to see her family. Maybe she'd plan a trip to one of places she'd always dreamt of going…Italy…or France…or Spain. Sighing as reality reared it familiar head, she allowed the dream bubble to burst.

She didn't even have a passport.

"You better turn over, you're going to burn," the deep voice was low and menacing and sent a chill up her warm spine. For a moment, she was reminded of gravel and sandpaper, though neither of those made her body respond so quickly or so feverishly.

Removing the hat from her face, she looked up, into the sun and at the gorgeous male standing over her. He had on just the white shorts now and the expanse of his strong chest took her breath away. It was sprinkled with salt and pepper hair that matched his temple, causing her to wonder just how old he was.

"I can't," she managed feebly.

"Why not?" He didn't try to hide the

amusement in his tone.

"Because," she sat up gingerly, holding a hand to her chest to avoid falling out of her very conservative one- piece swimsuit. "I can't reach my back to put sunscreen on it."

"No worries," he said, plopping down on the chair next to her. "Turn over, I'll do it."

Molly chewed on the inside of her lower lip as she considered his offer. Already she was treading on thin ice by being near him, but to have him touch her…that seemed entirely too dangerous and liberal for Molly Carson.

"Molly," he said, his voice low and meant for only her, "I'll be gentle". He spoke in a way that was kind and yet, provocative. She felt foolish for being so reluctant and decided to trust him. For now.

Carson had to look away once he got a glimpse of her tight little bottom as she turned over. He felt like a cad to be so turned on by such a sweet, innocent, that he nearly put down the SPF45 and ran. Almost.

His hands were both strong and gentle and his touch elicited a soft moan from Molly. It was heaven, having those hands spreading sunscreen on her back and down the back of each slender leg. She almost cried out when he was finished.

"How are you feeling?" He asked, trying to derail his line of thinking. She'd felt sweeter than he'd imagined as his large hand nearly covered two thirds of her back, and he almost convinced himself that he may be in bigger trouble than she.

"Better. You were right," she opened one eye to glance at him, "the food helped."

"You need lots of water too. I forgot to mention that."

"Oh, I've been drinking plenty of water today. I wouldn't want to get dehydrated in the sun."

Of course, he thought to himself with a smile. That would not be practical. Allowing himself an afternoon break, Carson stretched out on the lounge chair, adjusting the seat so he could gaze at the ocean.

"Uh. Er. Do you want me to put some sunscreen on you?" She was simply offering to reciprocate his kind gesture. Really. She prayed he said no.

"Nah. Thanks. I don't burn." Eyeing his deep, dark tan, Molly decided that he had no need of sunscreen like he said. He looked like he was born in the sun, he was so vital and healthy and tan.

"Are you Hispanic?" The politically correct ethnic reference came out of her mouth before she could stop it. *It's none of your business, Molly!* She was grateful that he could not see the color that rose to her cheeks.

His grin told her that he wasn't offended by her nosiness. "Portuguese and Italian."

"That's quite a combination," she smiled, her eyes closed and her head resting on her arms.

"I'm usually told that I'm hot-blooded."

"Well, I should think so. Which side is which?"

"My mother was Italian." At her nod, he lobbed the conversation back to her. "Let me guess your heritage…"

A blue eye popped open curiously as he pondered her with a long look up and down her body and then at her face.

She had a pixie-like face that was both delicate and stubborn at the same time. There was a faint sprinkle of freckles across her nose and cheekbones, though one had to look closely to see them. She had dimples at her cheeks and her eyes…well…"Irish and German."

Molly propped up on her forearms and stared at him with her mouth slightly open. "That's uncanny! How did you know?"

"It's a gift," he leaned over and intimately tucked a stray hair behind her ear, while she quickly tried to cover she cleavage view with a hand. His touch was like a blast of fire over her already heated body.

For several long moments he kept his face close and moved her hair around as he looked into her wide eyes. It wasn't that her hair was covering her shoulders, it was that he wanted to run her hair through his fingertips.

"You know, I'm not usually so remiss…and I really hate to say this. I'm so embarrassed," she was beginning to ramble, a habit that had started in her youth when she was nervous. "I hope you don't think that it hasn't been a pleasure to meet you, but…"

Thinking she was going to ask him to leave, Carson set one foot on either side of the chair to do just that. Until she uttered her next sentence.

"But I'm afraid I don't remember your name."

Grinning at the reminder of her inebriation the previous night, he happily supplied, "Carson".

"Car - Oh yes – now I remember! How could I forget, really? I mean, I told you that your first name is my last name, didn't I? I was amused by it, but then again I'm not accustomed to drinking alcohol. Not that it isn't amusing without the alcohol, but I think the alcohol made me forget…" She felt ridiculous now and couldn't seem to stop the flow of words out of her mouth.

"Yes, you did mention that. No worries. You just had a little to drink last night, that's all. You should enjoy yourself on vacation." He felt movement in his shorts at the memory of her breast touching his arm. It amazed him that such a sweet woman could elicit such a surge of lust in him.

"You say that a lot, don't you?"

Having forgotten what he just said, he raised an eyebrow. "What's that?"

" 'No worries'. You say that a lot."

"Well, I guess I do. And I don't. Worry, that is. I leave that up to the female population."

"It's true." He'd meant it as light humor, but Molly took him very seriously. She sighed. "We women do worry a lot."

"What do you worry about Nurse Molly Carson?" His voice was low and teasing and sent goosebumps down her spine.

"Things. My next job. Bills. Getting on a boat this week…"

"Are you looking for a job?" He'd wait to tackle the boat comment until he could think more about it.

"Yes…" *Roger.* Memories flooded her again, taking her off guard. "I'm currently between jobs." She tried to hide the catch in her voice, but was not able to.

"Did something happen at work, Molly?"

She wanted to tell him about Roger…confide in him - in someone - and hear words of comfort. But it seemed to minimize the situation by talking to a stranger about him, so she just nodded. "Yes. It ended badly, I guess you could say."

"I'm sorry to hear that. It's their loss then," he magnanimously lightened his tone to get her out of the funk he could feel her sinking into.

"No," she whispered, "it's my loss really."

Sensing that she didn't want to talk about it any more, he steered the conversation back on safer ground. "Now, about that boat…"

"Oh. Yes, well, I need to charter a boat sometime this week. That's all. I suppose I'll ask the Concierge."

Smiling, Carson offered, "I'd be happy to take you anywhere you want on my boat. Free of charge."

"Oh – I couldn't." She sat up and quickly covered her cleavage with her hand. "That's really very nice of you, but it's much too much of an imposition. You've been very kind to me already."

Touched by her protest, he put a hand on her shoulder. "It would not be an imposition. I'd love an excuse to take my boat out. Really."

"Well…" again she chewed on the inside of her lower lip, contemplating her next comment.

"Just say ok. Ok?"

"Ok." Relieved, she laid back down.

"There is one catch, however," Carson was quick to grab the opportunity.

Disappointment lit her face. "Oh. What is the catch?"

"You must have dinner with me tonight."

Yes! Oh, that would be delightful! She paused for a long moment before she shook her head. "I don't think that's a good idea…"

"Why not?" He didn't give her a chance to answer.

"You can make up for your abominable behavior last night." At her look of horror, he chuckled low and deep. "I'm just teasing. You were fine last night, but I didn't get to have dinner with you and I'm sorely disappointed."

"I – ah, well ok." She felt trapped and didn't know what else to say or do. He seemed genuinely interested in her company, so she supposed it couldn't hurt. But she would have to fight this growing attraction she was feeling for him. He couldn't possibly be interested in her for anything other than company. Perhaps he was lonely.

After a half hour of comfortable silence, Molly began to get restless. She turned, then turned again, unable to be comfortable anymore in the plush lounge chair.

Amused, Carson merely watched her struggle.

"I think I've had enough sun for today."

Not wanting his time with her to end, he inquired, "have you seen the water fall yet?"

"Waterfall? What waterfall?" Her look of pure delight made him grin.

"I'll take that as a no. The waterfall on the eastern side of the grounds. It's really quite beautiful."

"Actually, I haven't seen much of anything yet. I didn't exactly feel like sightseeing this morning."

She grinned at him, and he was rewarded with the small dimples on both cheeks. It was endearing. It was damn sexy.

"Well, let's go then! I'll give you a private tour of the Waverly Kauai Resort!"

Glad that he wasn't sick of her presence, Molly took his outstretched offered hand and gathered up her things.

She tied her beach wrap around her hips and when she reached to fold the towel, he took it from her hands. With a nod of his head, one of the bar stewards who had been serving poolside drinks was immediately at their side.

"Hello, Andy. Please take care of Miss Carson's towels, would you?"

Immediately the steward took both towels and was off before she could close her mouth from the protest that was on the tip of her lips.

"Wow. That's incredible service!" She was completely impressed, both with the fact that he knew the stewards name and that the steward was so quick to do his bidding. "I'll have to mention that on my comment card!"

She seemed very pleased and he still didn't feel the need to tell her that he knew all of his employees names, so he just let her have her delight. It made him smile.

Their tour of the huge grounds took almost two hours. He seemed to know every nook and cranny. Set upon a small hill adjacent to the beach, the design of the hotel seemed to mold the landscape around the buildings. There were long, winding paths that took one through areas of such lush gardens, that it was difficult to remember that around the next bend was another building or an outdoor restaurant or bar.

There were seven pool areas all together, some specifically designed for children, with rope swings and water slides. She was amazed that only several hundred yards away she had laid without hearing one peep from a playful child.

The design was magnificent in the way it seemed both expansive and private all at once. When he didn't suggest they go into the kitchen, she was almost disappointed.

He was an excellent tour guide, who allowed her the perfect amount of time to ask questions and stop to admire the view of this pool or that flower. He told her about the history of the island and the design and lengthy process of building the massive hotel. He delighted in telling her that the architecture was actually modeled after a Tahitian style that seemed to fit in this tropical location.

She was amazed by the hundreds of palm trees and couldn't stop looking up at their magnificence. The way they swished in the gentle breeze was a soothing reminder of the beauty of this tropical place.

When they reached the 200-foot waterfall in yet another secluded pool area, she let out a cry of delight. It was the most beautiful waterfall she'd ever seen. Well, actually, it was the only waterfall she'd ever seen in person. Even standing a good twenty feet away from it, she could feel the misty spray from where it pelted powerfully into the pool. She took a deep breath and closed her eyes for a moment.

"I've never seen anything more beautiful," she said with incredulous awe in her voice as she looked up at the flow of water bursting aggressively from the rocks, her hair flowing in massive curls behind her as her chin tipped up to the spray.

Carson had seen the transformation as they walked the grounds. Gone was the grief-stricken look and her face looked younger, softer. She was captivated by his words and asked intelligent, thought provoking questions that he thrilled in answering. Her eyes were warm with interest and an almost business like respect. He felt pulled to her now as she stared in pure, innocent wonder at this creation of his.

"Neither have I," he responded, his voice low and gruff as he took in every detail of her wide, appreciative eyes, her petite frame leaning against the safety rail and her hair, blowing behind her, down her back. She was all he wanted at that very moment.

She turned a radiant smile in his direction, as if thanking him personally for this miracle of beauty. He seized the opportunity and pulled her toward him by gently wrapping an arm around her waist.

"Haven't you ever seen a waterfall before?"

Molly wasn't allowed a moment to stiffen when he pulled her close and her body heated up the very instant their bodies collided. She had to lean back again to look at his face to see what this was all about.

Oh.

He was looking at her with fierce intensity and interest. It was a look she'd only seen manufactured in a movie when the leading man wanted to kiss the leading woman. It only took a moment for her to acknowledge that his eyes were searching her face for some kind of permission. She was terrified. She was exhilarated. This shouldn't happen, her mind warned her. Yet, she was hungry for what she prayed was coming next.

"No," she said softly. "I've never..."

The sun was beginning to set, causing dusk to settle on the water. It seemed so right, so perfect, that he kiss her then and there.

"Then you must be kissed at the waterfall, since it's your first time."

With one hand cradling her cheek, his head descended.

His lips were warm and gentle on hers. It was a soft kiss. Warm and kind at first. A gentle nibble. She tasted of mint gum and suntan lotion, and underneath it, he thought he could taste an innocence. It intoxicated him, made him greedy. He knew he should go slowly, but his mind and his body were battling a losing argument. He captured her lips in a long embrace, first the bottom lip and then the top trying with haste to satisfy the need he had to possess her in a single kiss. His hands found a home in her hair, weaving the soft tendrils between his fingers, while gently pulling her head back so that he could get closer; go deeper.

Molly joined the kiss after the initial surprise wore off and began doing a little tasting of her own. A groan from his throat encouraged her on and tentatively, she touched her tongue to his lips, drawing an imaginary line along its fullness.

Unable to hold back any longer, Carson pulled Molly so close that she could feel his hardness pressing against her belly. His tongue and lips launched a passionate invasion that seemed to penetrate all her good senses until she was clinging to him out of desperate, unknowing need.

Breaking away to taste her neck, he left her mouth aching for his. She sighed with a long rush of air she didn't realize she was keeping, as she felt every nerve in her body come alive. Molly felt herself drowning, losing herself in his passionate assault. She wanted to beg him to stop. She wanted to beg him not to stop.

At last, awareness of their surroundings penetrated his focused concentration on his companion's lips. He hadn't expected such a passionate response – neither from her nor from himself! He had to remind himself that they were in a public place where anyone could stumble upon them and he had to pull himself together.

With immense regret, he pulled his mouth away and simply held her in his strong arms, while he took long, deep breaths to clear his head. Already he was anticipating their next kiss…with any luck it would be only a few hours away.

Molly was glad he held her, because she thought for certain that her legs had left her somewhere back at the other pool.

"Carson," she whispered. Was that husky, sexy voice really hers?

Her intention was to tell him that it was inappropriate to behave this way while they were barely acquainted – had never even had a date! But she knew that her protest would bring his rumbling laughter and that like many other men, he probably thought of her as an aging spinster. It was old fashioned and dreary of her to think that way, especially since Roger had tried so hard to bring her into a more modern line of thinking.

Still, her body and her mind seemed disconnected as she murmured again, "Carson."

"I know, sweetness, I know." He held her face in his hands as he tenderly caressed her lips with his thumbs. Her eyes were wide with wonder and for a brief second he felt guilty for drawing her in. Like the wolf luring the lamb. But she was a grown woman and he was a healthy male. Surely she knew what to expect from a man like him?

Dismissing the guilty thoughts, Carson tried to collect himself - he was painfully aware of his arousal. After several minutes had gone by, he took her hand and said, "Come on."

They walked at a leisurely pace, back along the water toward the main pools of the hotel, their hands swinging casually together between their bodies, though the mild contact was like an electric current between them. They passed the bar where they'd met just the evening before and waved to Sam, who was closing it down for the night. A tall, beautiful woman watched them pass, with a polite smile and a nod in their direction.

Yearning for something to take her mind off of her body's heat, Molly tried to keep it light when she said, "are you hungry?"

His animal growl in response made her realize that that was the last thing to ask at this point, which made her giggle. Giggle? Practical Molly Carson giggled? That in itself made her giggle again. Was it possible that booze could have a flashback?

"Sorry. Bad choice of words."

"Would you like dinner?" He smiled at her seductively to which she swallowed hard.

"Yes," was all she could manage, though she doubted she would be able to eat anything just now. He walked her to her room and again pulled her close. She was afraid that if he tried to kiss her again, she might invite him in – something that she wouldn't dream of doing! It was preposterous…it was tempting.

So when he leaned down to kiss her, she put both hands on his chest and gave a strong shove. It did little to actually push him away. He smiled in amusement.

"I…well, I'll just need a half hour to get ready for dinner…" She pulled away and he let her. She looked at her watch and, tried to sound business-like, "shall I meet you downstairs at say…6:30?"

"I'll come here for you at 6:30," he corrected.

"Ok, well, then, see you at 6:30," she turned and fit her card key into the door, only she did it backwards and then dropped it on the ground. She was quite aware that he was watching her every move. With her back to him, she stooped to pick up the card and got a low whistle of appreciation. Standing back up abruptly, she finally managed to put the card in properly and opened the door.

"Ok. See you," she flashed a bright smile his way before shutting the door and leaning her back up against it.

Whew. She let out a deep breath and willed her body to return to normal, but rebelliously, her tummy still fluttered and her knees still felt weak. It was not a feeling she was accustomed to and she wasn't sure she liked it. She had little time to linger over this new dilemma and honestly, there was a part of her that didn't want to think it over too much anyway. So she focused on the next important issue at hand…what to wear?

The short man in his late twenties was known only as "the Kid", because he looked so young. After an uneventful flight, he rented a car and drove to a small motel that was no Waverly Hotel, but it was clean and cheap.

Once in his room, the Kid dug the watch out of his duffle bag so he could examine it more closely. It really did look like just a regular diving watch, but his contact told him he'd better guard it with his life. That was lame. Although he couldn't shake the feeling that someone was following him. Shaking it off, he decided it was time to get a beer. Nothing was going to happen for a few days so he may as well enjoy the island.

3

Fifteen minutes later, Carson sat at the indoor bar with a view overlooking the ocean. Sam was serving and automatically handed him his usual Corona.

"Moonlighting, Sam?" He was aware that Sam had already worked a full shift at The Dock Bar.

"Yes, sir. I'm covering for Tom who had to pick up his old lady from the airport. He should be back soon."

Looking Carson up and down, Sam noted. "You look like you've got a hot date, Mr. Waverly."

"Sam, when are you going to stop that Mr. Waverly nonsense and just call me Carson?"

At the shrug from the bartender, Carson changed the subject to the one thing that he'd been unable to get off of his mind all day.

Molly.

"I'm taking Miss Carson to dinner tonight."

"Woooooweee," Sam shook his head. "It's gonna take more than a few Blue Hawaiians to thaw that ice,

Mr. W."

"Oh I don't know Sam. I think I'm halfway there." Satisfied with his progress so far, Carson savored the sip of his beer and winked at his friend.

"She's not as cold as you'd think."

"Not your usual type, if you don't mind my saying so."

"You're right. Maybe that's why I'm attracted to her." They shared a chuckle.

Changing the subject again, Carson looked closely at Sam. "How's the family?"

"Ok, I guess. My wife's holding her own at the moment."

"The kids?"

"Feisty and disagreeable, but that's to be expected with teenagers."

"If you need anything, Sam, you will let me know, right?"

"You've already done so much…" The paid time off; paying for childcare during the surgery and then taking on the medical bills. Sam would not be able to accept any more from his boss and friend.

"You're one of my most loyal employees, Sam. I'm happy to help. I expect you to let me know, ok?" Carson tried to muster a stern look, but Sam wasn't fooled.

"Sure, Mr. W, but don't worry. Everything's fine."

Carson was thinking about Sam as he rode the elevator to pick up Molly. Sam's wife had recently had a mastectomy followed by intense chemotherapy for breast cancer and Sam had lovingly taken care of her and their here children.

He was an amazing man, Carson thought, and

briefly wondered if he'd ever have the strength to care for an ailing wife with such love and devotion. He didn't like the answer that came to him at the same time the elevator opened.

Probably not, especially considering that he planned never to get married.

Carson must have had a frown on his face when Molly answered the door, because her smile of greeting faded into a look of concern.

"Carson? Are you ok?"

"Yes, I was just thinking about business, that's all."

Changing his mood, he smiled at her, taking in her black, rayon sundress and the heels that gave her several more inches. Her hair was swept up into a loose bun, with several loose strands framing her face. She looked classy and somewhat sophisticated. And now she was looking burdened.

"You're beautiful," he said with all the charm he could muster.

"Well, passable. Thank you," she appreciated his attempt to cheer her after she opened the door to his wretched expression. She would get to the bottom of that eventually – if she got the opportunity and he didn't get completely bored by her this evening.

Grabbing her purse, she took his offered arm. Here we go, she thought.

Dinner was an unexpected, romantic surprise. While she thought they'd get in his car and drive into town, she found that she was mistaken. They walked leisurely holding hands along the water until they came to a secluded area of lawn about 100 yards from the hotel.

A small table sat waiting for them, surrounded with just enough tiki torches to add an additional air of romance. The table was set with white linen and china, and a coconut candle surrounded by Hawaiian flowers made the centerpiece. It was exquisite.

Gasping with delight, Molly turned into Carson's arms.

"It's spectacular!" She breathed with little need to hide her enthusiasm.

He chuckled at her childlike excitement and kissed the tip of her nose.

"I'm glad you like it."

"Aloha," the expectant waiter said as he held the chair for Molly.

They sat closely so that they could both enjoy the moonlit ocean as it gently lapped waves onto the shore. The menu was predetermined, so they began with cocktails and jumbo shrimp as an appetizer. The shrimp were almost as large as a child's hand and when Carson held it up to her mouth, she happily took the end between her lips.

It was delicious.

She was delicious, he thought.

Having dropped some of the primness after spending time with him, Molly now exuded a subtle sexuality that suited her. She still appeared rather innocent, but her eyes gave away her attraction to him and that moved him more than he was willing to admit. Tonight he hoped to explore that sexuality, perhaps right here in the moonlight.

Dinner was one delectable Hawaiian dish after another, until sharing the macadamia nut crème brulee seemed impossible. But she just had to try a bite, so she agreed.

"Tell me about your family," Carson invited, hoping she might shed some light on the reason for her grief.

"There's not much to tell, really. My parents still live in Idaho. I have one older brother, Robert, and he's a farmer in Montana. Oh. I guess the term is 'rancher' – I always get that wrong."

"So you're all alone in San Francisco?" His voice was kind and she willed herself not to feel the pang of sadness over Roger.

"Well, I have – had – no, have friends there." She did have a few friends, after all. Some of the nurses that she worked with before working directly for Roger still kept in touch and they went out together now and then. But her best friend, her confidant, had been Roger since the moment she moved into the drafty old apartment in North Beach.

Carson watched the flood of emotion that lighted her face and watched her just as quickly mask it. Tonight was not about her grief, he reminded himself. It was about pleasure.

"Do you go visit your family very often?"

"Not lately. I mean, for the past couple of years I've been wrapped up in work, but I will probably go see them now that...."

"Now that you're between jobs?" He tried to help her – God knows he wanted to help her, but something told him she just wasn't ready. He willed himself to be patient.

"Yes, exactly." Relieved to be off the subject

and searching for something – anything else to talk about, Molly blurted out a question to avoid the current topic. "How come you're not married?"

He pulled back in his chair and sat silently staring at his glass of wine for a long time. So long, that Molly thought he wouldn't answer.

"I'm not the marrying type, Molly." Carson struggled with what should have been a simple answer.

I haven't met the right woman. I've been busy with my career. Both seemed like logical excuses if he were a normal man. But he wasn't normal and he didn't want to lie to this woman. Suddenly it seemed very important to him that she understand what he was saying and accept him for who he was. Or was not. Then it would be her choice to move forward, absolving him of any guilt.

"Oh." Molly felt her heart sink. It was impossible that she should even consider more than a passing liaison with this man, but for whatever reason, she had begun to hope that their first date might turn into a second…and then a third. And maybe, just maybe, there was more to this casual meeting than what the signs seemed to be telling her.

Yet here he was being totally honest with her – she couldn't blame him for being so blunt. She must appear to be an old-fashioned woman pinning her hopes on this dashing, successful bachelor. How silly of her to hope! And with a single sentence, those hopes of a future with this man had just been permanently shut down.

"I'm sorry – it's none of my business – "

"Molly – " he interrupted the expected flurry of words with his curt use of her name. He tried to look kind and keep his voice level, but firm. He wouldn't let this topic reveal too much of himself. There was no room for negotiation. "I travel all the time, Molly." His tone was gentler as he tried to find words to explain himself.

"I don't put down permanent roots in any one place for long. I don't want to be responsible for anyone but myself. I don't want to wake up beside the same woman for the rest of my life. It's not who I am. I just live each moment as it is. That's it. No strings. No worries."

Molly felt a lump in her throat so she reached for her water. His honesty was admirable, even if it disappointed her to hear it. But why should she care? Couldn't he be just a little island fling for her? A distraction? Roger would applaud the very idea of it and urge her to take advantage of this delectable offering. Part of her was tempted to do exactly that. It would be so glamorous to be able to have an affair with this gorgeous, interesting man and move on as if it didn't matter.

The problem was that everything mattered to Molly. She didn't attach herself lightly to people. She loved. And she stayed. But she knew danger when she saw it and she must put a wall around her heart where this man was concerned. The question was, could she walk away now before she got in over her head?

"I'm sorry, Carson, I should mind my own business." She lightened her tone considerably and said, "of course you like your life the way it is. Not everyone wants to get married and have a family. It's nice that you know yourself so well. I hope you find happiness, Carson, I really mean it." She touched his hand with sincere kindness, even if she had pulled back emotionally from him.

He felt both responses. It was almost as if suddenly there was a wall separating them, even if she only slightly straightened her spine.

Never before had he felt like such a cad. And he hadn't even slept with her yet! It would almost be easier if she caused a scene, as he was used to. The conversation they were having was not foreign to him. In fact, he often spoke the same words to women he dated, but not until after he had slept them and they became too clingy.

Reactions were typical and quite predictable. First there was the surprise, accompanied by soft exclamations of "what do you mean?" Then when he articulated exactly what he meant (because he apparently hadn't been clear enough) she would let her claws out and berate him for using her.

He was good at soothing ruffled feathers, however and soon anger changed into the "knowing" look that he hated the most. Each of them thought she could *change* him, though her self-satisfied condescension only lasted a couple of months until she realized she couldn't.

He tried to end the affair in an amiable way, but there were always hurt feelings and disappointment. He regretted that he hurt his lovers, but it couldn't be avoided. At least he had the piece of mind that he was honest from the beginning. Just as he was with Molly.

Part of him felt relieved that she let him off the hook so easily and he tried to resume the playful atmosphere. He turned his hand in hers and brought it to his lips for nibbling as he looked into her eyes with an intense smolder.

"I know what would give us both pleasure right now," he said intensely. He watched as she battled whatever arguments that only she was privy to in her beautiful head. Doubt. Confusion. Uncertainty. She was so easy to read and he almost chuckled as she remained rigid under his administrations.

Molly was beside herself with a mixture of feelings and thoughts. He was spelling it out for her quite clearly. An affair. Her back remained stiff and she held her free hand against her chest as he continued to seduce her with his lips on her open palm.

It seemed most ridiculous that this handsome, virile man could be attracted to her – Molly Carson, registered nurse from Idaho – when it was obvious that he could pick any woman that he wanted. Perhaps he was simply amusing himself with her. She must appear to be an easy conquest for him, and he was quite confident that he would succeed. She was relatively confident he would succeed also, because there was no denying how extremely attracted she was to him.

His life was so much bigger than the small life she had known, a reminder that she was out of her element. But wasn't that the very thing which Roger chastised her for at every turn - to change her element? To become more worldly? To enjoy life while she was fortunate to live without physical or monetary limitations?

She wasn't ready to decide just yet. Coward. Well, yes, she admitted to herself. She gently pulled her hand away and settled back into her companionable questioning.

"What do you do for a living?"

Carson accepted her ploy to keep things on a more comfortable ground – for now- and answered her easily. "I'm an architect." It was the truth, even if it was only half of it.

"Really?!" She was delighted at his response. The idea that someone could be so creative and apply it in such a way intrigued her. "Oh that's so exciting! I'm fascinated with architecture and the creative differences of each building and how it impacts our environment! What do you design? Houses? Offices?"

"Hotels…and houses…whatever projects I'm interested in pursuing."

"Hotels?" It only took a second for her to put it all together. "You designed this hotel, didn't you?" At his nod, she almost squealed with delight. "No wonder you know every nook and cranny. Wow! I'm so impressed. You are very talented, Carson!" She laid a meaningful hand on his arm, then slowly pulled back as she felt the electricity of their contact.

His eyes seemed to darken momentarily, unnerving her into continuing the half-hearted ramble.

"You said you had connections – well, no wonder! You probably know everyone on staff here! Of course, you probably get a really great deal to stay here, don't you? Oh. But then you said you have a home here, so you'd probably stay there, right?"

He leaned over and held her face in his hand, even as she continued to babble. At last, he put his lips to hers, cutting her words off. "You were rambling," he teased.

"I know. I do that when I'm nervous," she held her tongue then, though every part of her wanted to ramble some more. But his lips were still very close to hers and she was having a difficult time breathing.

"It seems we've found a way to stop it." He kissed her again, his lips lingering for a long, precious moment. "We'll call it 'kissing therapy'."

"We could write a book about it," she giggled

softly, his lips still only inches away.

"We'll make a fortune," he agreed, his eyes intensely staring at her parted lips.

His mouth took hers then, with a fierceness she had not experienced before. He was no longer testing and tasting. He possessed her, demanded her response and delved into the farthest reaches of her soul. While he was not hurting her, he was also not exactly gentle. If there had been any doubt as to his intentions, they were kissed away in that instant.

Her response was tentative at first, but as he pulled her lower lip into his, she felt herself give in. When his tongue sought hers, she gasped and then allowed it. Her senses were reeling with desire and an alarm was going off in her head. But for a moment – a glorious, delicious moment – she let herself enjoy this man's possessive kiss.

At last when she found the strength, she pushed him away. Barely aware that the dishes had been cleared and they were now alone in this very secluded place by the beautiful ocean…well, panic nearly took hold as a voice inside her head warned her, "You're out of your league here".

Breathing hard, she looked at the tablecloth, unable to meet his gaze. Her body was betraying her, and she had to will it to shut up. She wanted him too, darn it.

"Wait," she breathed when she was able to. He leaned in for another taste when she put a hand to his chest, then quickly drew it back when she encountered his muscular pecks. "Just wait."

She pushed back from the table and stood, moving toward the ocean to distance herself from him. She knew it wouldn't keep him away, but at least she had a moment to think.

"What are you afraid of, Molly?" His voice was deep and seductive and only inches behind her. She could feel the heat from his body as he moved closer, but didn't touch her.

She thought back to his words earlier that day. No, they hadn't made love….yet. A shiver cascaded down her spine. What *was* she afraid of? She had to be honest with herself, because somehow, she knew this was a pivotal moment in her life. A chance to break out of her safe little world and live…as Roger had always wanted for her.

And here was the most handsome, interesting, sexy man she'd ever met and he was telling her that he wanted *her.* The idea should delight her, not send her screaming from the scene.

Perhaps in a few days, she might feel differently, so she mustered up the courage to turn and look him in the eye. "I need more time," she apologized with her eyes. "I'm not good at this. I must seem like a complete country bumpkin. I'm sure the other women you date are much more – more...cosmopolitan."

When he just stood staring at her as she struggled with words and emotion, she sighed and looked at her feet. "Please don't be angry with me."

He wasn't angry. How could he be angry at her standing there looking so tormented? He wanted to take away her anxiety, to bring back her smile.

He reached a hand out and cupped her chin. "I won't apologize for wanting you, Molly. You're a beautiful, sexy woman." He ignored the roll of her eyes in disbelief. "I will give you the time you need. When you're ready, you let me know, but don't take too long. Vacations end."

Some of the fear left her eyes. "But in the meantime, I will continue to kiss you. I can't help myself. But we'll stop when you say to stop. Ok?"

She nodded and gulped at the same time, and her lips parted to receive another onslaught of his aggressive passion. But his kiss was gentle again and did not demand anything of her. And it ended without her pushing him away.

He leaned his forehead into hers and said very softly, "What did he do to you, Molly?"

"Who?"

"The man that hurt you. The one that obviously gave you a good dose of fear of men."

"It's not like that," she tried to explain. How could she possibly tell him that there had been no man…that her fear was simply lack of experience and the unknown?

"Tell me." He took her hand and turned her back toward the hotel. He was inviting her to share a part of her that she had only shared with one other person. Roger.

"I can't. It's not that gloomy, though, really. I just need some time to – to – adjust to this idea of a - an affair."

The idea sounded naughty and shameful when she lowered her voice and whispered it from her prim lips and he found himself insulted. What did she think that he was only in it for the sex?

The quick flare of temper quickly vanished when he realized that sex was exactly what he was in it for, so there was no need to be a hypocrite. Hadn't he just told her that all he had to offer her or any woman was an affair of sexual delight. A physical connection focused in the here and now. He was a temporary part of her vacation. And they both knew it.

She was just speaking plainly about it, which he had to admire.

"I see," he said, hoping she'd go on.

Feeling inspired by his understanding, Molly persisted. "Anyway, I just have to get used to the idea. I've never been one for…for…dalliances." Or for talking about it, for crying out loud!

"But you want to." He pulled her into his arms again and nibbled at her ear while he could feel her calculating her words. He wouldn't give her the chance to speak them. "You want to so badly, you can taste it."

"I don't – "

"Don't deny it, Molly. We've got chemistry and it would be good. But I understand you."

He said it so knowingly that Molly swallowed the dryness in her throat to ask, "understand what about me?"

"You probably sit home at night wishing for romance. Life. Adventure. You dream that someday a man will sweep you off your feet and give you the kind of life you hope for. But you've always been too afraid to reach out and make it happen for yourself."

"How dare y-"

"Am I right?" His voice was menacing and low against her ear.

She tried to pull away. "Yes."

"And now here you are with a man who desires you very much. I can give you adventure and pleasure, but you are afraid."

He took a step closer to her, his musky scent ruining her concentration.

"Isn't that what you want, Molly? A change from your boring, chaste existence? A little excitement? A little passion?"

"You don't know me at all!" Her words were unconvincing as he stepped forward again, holding her gaze captive as he ran a finger along her jaw.

"I know you, Molly. I know what you want," he spoke seductively, his eyes now on her pouting lips.

"You need a man who can show you exactly what real pleasure is. To make love to you until your head caves in. To taste every inch of your body. To take you to places you've never dared to go. You want me, Molly, but you're too afraid. I wonder, though. Are you afraid of me? Or are you afraid of yourself?"

"Is it so weird that I may not be interested in sleeping with a man I barely know?"

She pulled free from his embrace and turned away from him. Embarrassment and fury warred within her as she struggled to find the words. He was right, darn him, and she felt foolish that she was so transparent.

When she whirled back to face him, he was a few feet away, his foot propped up on a large rock. His smile was smug. He was proud of himself for pegging her so successfully!

She tipped her chin defiantly and tossed out, "I'm not afraid!"

For an instant, he reconsidered his comments and thought, perhaps he'd read it completely wrong.

He walked purposely toward her and cupped her face in his large hand. "Molly – are you – involved with someone back home?"

Her mouth fell open at his question, but then she realized that it was quite possible that she was.

How would he have known? Though why she'd be here on vacation alone or having dinner with a handsome man certainly wasn't an indication of her having a boyfriend.

"NO!" She practically shouted at him, her surprise was so great. "How could you think that I would be here with you if I was?" Was the world really that warped?

"I didn't think you were – and now that you mention it, it was a ridiculous question. I'm sorry. But it would have explained your reluctance to make love with me."

Pulling away, Molly felt both violated and complimented at the same time. Then it occurred to her…"Are you?"

"Am I what?"

"Are you involved with anyone?" Her tongue felt heavy in her mouth as she asked the question. It was definitely possible. What was the modern term? An open relationship? If he was commitment phobic then that type of relationship would suit him. Oh boy. It was one thing to read romance stories about this world, but to actually be a part of it completely baffled her.

"Not at the moment, no." She felt him pull away even though he didn't move a muscle.

"You're a rambler," she tried not to sound disgusted, because in reality, she admired the fact that he took so freely what was probably offered quite often. He most likely hung out at this hotel so he could have short, meaningless relationships with vulnerable women on vacation. And then he'd move on to his next location. Rambler was only one word that described him. Rogue. Womanizer. Confirmed bachelor.

"A Rambler? What is this, the 1800s?" When she blushed at his mockery, he sighed.

"I believe in living in the moment, Molly. In enjoying life right here, right now." He didn't understand why he felt the need to drive his point home, but her reaction to him mattered.

She couldn't speak, nor could she look at him.

Carson said in a low voice, "It's all I've got to give at this point in my life."

When she looked up directly into his eyes, she returned the question softly, "what did *she* do to you?"

"Who?"

"Whatever woman it was that made you afraid of being loved."

Anger sparked inside him and he pulled away from her to face the ocean. "You're mistaken," he said just loud enough for her to hear. "There was no woman. I am who I am. That's all."

"Was it the fact that your mother died when you were so young?" Her voice held compassion and sympathy and was completely without venom. Briefly, he hated her for it.

"That's so typical of a woman to try to rationalize my personality. I am who I am and I'm not going to change."

She understood. It hurt her on his behalf, but she understood. She walked up to him and laid a small hand on his wide back. For whatever reason, she wasn't willing to risk her heart to this stranger on this night – perhaps never. They both knew it.

"Thank you for dinner, Carson. It was lovely."

Her classy dismissal left him feeling like a real lowlife. He was used to being the one to control the pace and outcome of his relationships. Funny, not only was she out of her element, but he was too.

She turned to walk back to the hotel, when he called out to her, causing her to turn around.

"I'll walk you to your room." His offer was only half-hearted.

"No, thank you. I'll be fine. Good night." Her tone was dismissive and he accepted her rejection of his offer with some relief. Perhaps it was better this way.

When Molly reached the lighted pathway past the first pool, the tall, beautiful woman whom she'd seen earlier stepped out of the shadows. She wore an evening gown made of silky, subtly tropical material. It hung from one sculpted shoulder and crossed over her ample chest and dripped down to the floor with long slit all the way up her elegant legs to her hip. She had exotic eyes and a lush, full mouth with perfect white teeth.
She smiled at Molly and offered her a hand.

"Miss Carson?" she inquired, her voice soft and sultry. She was everything that Molly wasn't, which made her feel frumpy and clumsy.

Cautiously, Molly took her offered hand. "Yes?"

"I hope that everything meets with your expectation."

She was speaking of the hotel and it was then that Molly noticed the brass nametag pinned to the meager material of her gown.

"Why yes, it's a beautiful hotel. How did you know my name?"

"It's my job to know guests here." She smiled warmly, even if she was looking past her to the path from which she came.

"Oh. What is your job?" Still not sure why this gorgeous creature had singled her out, she was hoping to get to the bottom of it so that she could return to her room and contemplate the evening's events.

"I'm Leilani, the Amenities Director."

"That's nice," Molly was distracted by the fact that the woman continued to watch the path. "Are you looking for someone?"

Her beautiful features softened into an affectionate expression, her eyes gazing down bashfully. "I'm looking for Carson."

Molly's mouth opened in response and then clamped shut forcefully. "I…he…"

Leilani's eyes were wide with curiosity. "Did you see him?"

Finally finding her voice, Molly stood straighter, though she still seemed like a dwarf compared to this amazon, and wiped a crisp hand down the front of her sundress as if that would make her look more put together.

A stab of jealousy had her answering matter-of-factly, "I just had dinner with him down the path there."

Leilani looked her up and down with an amused air of condescension and then clearly dismissed her. "Oh. Well, since your 'dinner' is already over, I'll go look for him. I have a question that only he can answer."

She smirked as she attempted to brush past Molly.

Feeling oddly defensive, Molly stepped in front of her. "Dinner is already over because I ended the evening," she smiled secretively and flipped her hair off her shoulders, unaware that she could bear such claws and continued, "even though Carson tried to persuade me to stay. You may not want to approach him now…I left him in quite a state."

Obviously not threatened in the least, Leilani chuckled, "Relax, Miss Carson. I just have a business question for him." Though her words defied her body language, she informed Molly, "He's too old for me anyway. He's more like a…an uncle that I'm fond of. So you can rest assured that I'm not going after him the way that you are – I mean that you think I am."

Relaxing somewhat, Molly pulled her feline instincts back and smiled at Leilani.

"Well, I'm certainly not interested in Carson for anything other than friendship, so I wouldn't care if you were."

Leilani cocked her exotic head, an act that Molly was certain she perfected while looking in the mirror, it was so perfectly, innocently sensual.

"Of course I don't think you're interested in Carson! Besides, you're not exactly the usual type of woman that he goes after."

Molly couldn't figure out what this woman wanted. She seemed deceptively nice one moment, but her words cut into Molly the next. She hated herself for asking, but she couldn't stop herself.

"And what type of woman does he usually 'go after'?"

With a small wave of her hand indicating her type of physique, she tossed out, "well, taller, for one thing and I think his last two conquests were international models."

Seeing Molly's frown, she reached down and touched her shoulder comfortingly. "Don't worry, dear. You're better off without him. He's a heartbreaker, for sure! I'm sure you're not used to that."

Molly swallowed the lump that had lodged itself in her throat and attempted a careless smile. "I know. That's why I'm not with him now."

"Of course! No worries," she said mockingly as she continued down the path. "Enjoy your evening."

Molly didn't answer because she was concentrating every thought on moving her legs forward, toward the hotel, not back toward the beach. She would have liked to see Leilani's approach to Carson. *No worries.* Why did everyone keep saying that?

4

Make love. That's what he'd said. The idea was so delicious and tempting that Molly was unable to sleep at two in the morning. Her Idaho upbringing warred with the years spent in liberal San Francisco.

She was certain that her idea of making love was quite different than Carson's. For him the simple words described an extra-curricular activity, but for Molly, she didn't use the word 'love' lightly.

However, if she decided she was able to wrap her mind around the idea of an affair, she would have to carefully guard her heart. She was out of her element with a man such as Carson and every instinct beneath the tingling sensations his attention wrought, screamed "run!"

Yet it was those tingling sensations she could not ignore. And the nagging voice in her head which continued to remind her of her desire for adventure.

It irked her that he had so accurately pinpointed her deepest longings in merely a day. No one had a right to be that perceptive and then to presumably recount their opinions.

It left her feeling oddly vulnerable. And hot in the very depths of her body.

Carson went over and over the evening's conversation in his head and couldn't decide where exactly it had begun to go downhill. Sitting on the balcony of his penthouse suite smoking a cigar, he sipped at the glass of brandy. It was a beautiful night – seldom was there any other kind of evening on Kauai – but his thoughts were not on the view or the climate.

Molly.

He was afraid that he had assumed too much and spoken out of turn. He had no right to relate his observations of her, but the words were out of his mouth before he could take them back. The way that she bristled made him believe that he was probably on target and that she was afraid. And she had read him just as easily, driving to the core of his issues quite simply.

"Whatever woman it was that made you afraid of being loved." She was right on that level, though she had the wrong female. The only woman that ever hurt him was his stepmother, Eunice, that bitch. But his wounded ego would not allow him to drudge up old, buried ghosts.

This was about Molly.

Why wasn't she what she appeared to be? Chaste. Proper. A cold fish. No, she was none of those things. Well, maybe proper. But her body had come alive in his arms and her sweetness penetrated his defenses to the core. She had pressed into him like the passionate woman he was discovering her to be. He wanted her with a force he had never felt before and now he had blown it.

It was for the best, though, because he meant what he'd said. The only thing he had to offer was the present. There was no future for them together, so he put it out there for her to deal with. And she did. She walked away. Her mother would surely be proud.

The Kid cut through The Waverly Hotel on his way back to his dirty room. All day he'd felt like someone was watching him and it gave him the damned creeps. Can't a guy just have a few drinks in the bar in peace between drop-offs? But he couldn't shake the feeling there was someone there. He'd better get back to his room and see if the watch was still in the safe.

5

The next morning produced a cranky, tired Molly Carson. Cursing herself a thousand times over for the missed opportunity, Molly got up early and decided to go for a run on the beach. She really wasn't a runner, but isn't that what hip, modern women were supposed to do?

It turned out that running on the beach was much more romantic than it was practical, and she found that she twisted her ankle a quarter of a mile into her run. She had to limp back to the lobby, where a compassionate concierge offered to get her a doctor. She waved him away, insisting she was fine, it was just a sprain and that she just needed to rest it a bit.

She made her way back to her room, careful to use the wall for support. Once there, however, she realized she was somewhat stranded, since she had difficulty walking on the injured foot and it was beginning to swell. Muttering every bad word she could think of —and even a few she never used – Molly gave in and called the kind concierge.

"We'll send someone up right away, Miss

Carson," the older gentleman picked up the phone to dial the in-house doctor, but Carson stopped him.

"Mr. Waverly, sir, I didn't see you standing there." He was obviously flustered despite being in Carson's employ for five years now.

"Hello Gus. Does Miss Carson need something?"

"Yes, sir. It seems she's twisted her ankle on the beach and is in need of medical attention. I was just calling Dr. Smith now."

Very good, Gus. I'll take an icepack to her room in the meantime. I think the Doc is on the golf course."

"Ok, sir. Let me get her room number for you."

"I know what room she's in, Gus."

He walked away from a blushing concierge, whose response to his boss's knowledge of Miss Carson's room number was a mischievous smile.

Gus's daughter stood nearby witnessing the exchange with a frown. She'd never seen Carson jump to do a guest's bidding the way he had for frumpy Miss Carson. She would have to watch a little more carefully from now on.

Molly hopped on one foot to answer the knock at the door and had to admit that she was impressed at such a speedy response from the doctor. She was surprised but not disappointed, however, when Carson stood on the other side of the door with an ice pack and a first aid kit. Her body instantly responded to him with a tummy flutter and weakened knees.

Embarrassed that he should see her clumsy behavior, she tried sarcasm on for size and quipped, "What, are you a doctor too?" Nope. It didn't suit her.

Without an answer or a response to her sarcasm, he was on her and tipped her into his arms, lifting her from the ground in an easy swoop, eliciting an unladylike squeal from Molly. How did he do that with the items in his hands?

"Naw. But I do know first aid." He deposited her on the large bed and took a seat next to her, causing the bed to sink considerably. He was not a small man, she noted.

"Let's see."

"I just need an ace bandage and a little ice and I'll be as good as new!" She showed a brave face, but the fact was she'd never so much as broken a nail in her life and she found that she was a wimp when it came to the pain. Is this how her patients felt when they came in with injuries? She suddenly felt a fresh wave of compassion for every cut she tended and sprain she wrapped.

He repeated himself a little more forcefully this time as he said, "let's see."

Reluctantly, she let him take her foot in his large hands and carefully examine it from every angle.

"Looks like a sprain," he commented, all business. But his touch defied his tone. Her foot looked small and delicate in his large, tan hands as he took his time to look it over. His thumb was perched just at the curve of her arch, holding it securely. She felt a ripple of desire flow through her at his intimate touch.

As if he sensed her reaction to him, he looked up into her eyes and smiled gently.

"Yep, I think it's definitely a sprain."
Color had crept up to her cheeks because it seemed as if he could look right into her thoughts.

Changing the train of her thinking, she

whispered hoarsely, "How do you know?"

The humor of his assumed authority did not escape her and how he felt he should tell her – a trained nurse – what was wrong with her foot! Of course it was a sprain. She stifled the giggle that threatened.

"Because it's not swollen enough to be a break. I had plenty of broken bones as a kid to know the difference."

"Oh."

"I'll just wrap it up for you and we can put some ice on it. I think there's some Tylenol in here somewhere."

He rummaged through the kit, careful not to look her in the eyes.

"Actually, Motrin would be best," she hated to sound bossy, but it really would help with the swelling.

Gingerly, he wrapped her foot in an ace bandage as she watched helplessly. Did he purposely run a rough hand up her calve as he lifted her foot onto his lap?

"That's very kind of you," she started, but he merely shrugged.

"No worries. I wouldn't want you to sue me – I mean the hotel or anything."

"I would never sue someone for my own clumsiness! I think people that do are loathsome!" "Who uses words like loathsome?" He said it mostly to amuse himself, but regretted it the moment it was out of his mouth, because he felt her tense up.

"I'm just kidding."

"You're right." Her spine straightened and arms were crossed angrily. "I'm a dowdy old maid, that's what I am."

Well, she really sounded like a spoilt brat, but he

was not about to comment on that.

"Right!" He snorted out a laugh at the vision he got at that notion. "You're hardly dowdy and you are definitely not old."

"You're just being polite."

"How old are you?"

"I don't think it's any of your – " realizing that again she sounded dowdy and prude, she cut herself off with a grumpy "27."

With his task finally complete, he looked up into her worried eyes. "It's only fair that I tell you too...I'm 35."

"Oh." She knew he was older than she, but not by so many years.

"Does it bother you very much?" His tone was teasing and light. With the wrapping of her foot complete, his hand lingered on her exposed toes, where he explored her foot with an absent caress.

"Of course not. Why should it?"

Of course not, he thought. She wanted nothing to do with him now, so age was hardly an issue. His smile wavered.

"You probably want to stay off this – at least for today. I'll still ask the doc to come see you when he gets back to the hotel."

"I'm sure you have plenty to do – you really must not worry about me."

"Of course I must. You're a very important customer here."

His easy smile was – well, it was beautiful. She was almost certain he knew it.

Glancing around the room, he noticed a small, wallet-sized picture of a handsome man, at least forty years old, sitting next to a metal urn. "Who's that?"

He found himself asking.

"Oh. A friend," she didn't know what else to say, because the pain came back to her in a rush, clogging her throat with emotion.

Carson picked up and looked at the picture for a long time, not missing the affection and pain in her voice. Perhaps she *was* involved with someone, though two days ago she said she wasn't. A bad breakup would explain a lot of her issues, though it seemed very strange to him that a woman would bring her ex-boyfriend's picture on vacation. So who was he? She wasn't exactly forthcoming with information.

"Who?"

"Roger," she whispered the name as if she were committing sacrilege to say it out loud.

"I see." A stab of jealousy surprised him and he put the picture down none too gently. The room felt as if it were closing in on him, and for a brief second he got the urge to run. Ridiculous. He'd let her have her secrets…for now. He certainly had no right to pry.

A knock came at the door and Carson rose to answer it on her behalf. It was the doctor, who rushed in with his bag.

"Hello Carson! I heard you covered for me while I was…er…on the course."

Carson slapped him on the back. "No worries, doc. Hopefully I didn't do too much damage."

Carson took the opportunity to exit as the doctor unwrapped Molly's foot.

She heard the door click shut before she realized he'd gone, leaving her deflated. He may not be right for her…he may not want a relationship…but he was interesting and sexy and kind and smart. And his absence made the hotel room seem too empty. Oh dear.

The doctor agreed with her and Carson's assessments and offered her the use of the hotel wheelchair, if she so desired. She bristled at the idea and thanked him anyway.

"How long do I have to stay off of it?" she asked.

"At least a day. See how you feel. If you're anxious to get out and about, I could probably scour up some crutches for you."

"No, resting for a day or two will be fine."

"If it starts to feel better when you put pressure on it, then it's healing. Just do what you can. Call me if you need me," he cheerily left her to sulk over her sore foot.

Her patience lasted only a few hours before the boredom set in. She had nothing to read and she really wasn't much of a TV person. Still, she flipped through channels to see what people watched during the day. There was what she figured was a "talk show", but everyone seemed to be yelling and two of the people even broke out into a fistfight! On another channel, a woman was telling her cousin that she was carrying his baby but couldn't tell anyone it was his because she was in love with his brother. There were so many channels to choose from! Finally, she settled on the discovery channel, where a group of doctors were touring South Africa. It put her to sleep.

When she awoke at four o'clock, she was ravenous and, though she had read the room service menu at least a dozen times, she still didn't know what she wanted. She wasn't used to such indulgences as room service, though Roger would have howled at the idea of her being worried about money. Thanks to him, she would never have a money worry again.

By five her stomach was growling so rebelliously that she called down to order the biggest cheeseburger they could make – make it a double - fries, a salad and a fudge brownie for dessert.

Again she had to hobble to answer the door – something she was getting good at. Seeing her wrapped foot, the server asked her what happened. She motioned for him to put the food tray on the bed and mumbled something about that darned sand not being any place for people to run.

He grinned in response. She didn't know what exactly he thought was so amusing.

"Just give us a call when you want us to remove your tray."

"Ok. Thank you very much!"

She managed to get herself back to the bed and dove into the food with a vengeance. It was delicious and she almost ate every drop.

At eight, another knock sounded on the door and Molly didn't think she could make the trek now, after her belly was full, but she shouted, "just a minute" and hobble-walked to the door.

It was Carson and she fell just a little bit in love with him when she saw what he brought…magazines, books and an old, worn out cane.

"Carson!" She allowed him to pass her and dump the contents onto the bed. Then he turned to her and handed her the cane.

"Give it a whirl," he encouraged and the cane aided her in hobbling much better than she had before.

"Where did you get this?" she asked,

embarrassed that he should witness her awkward first steps with it.

"I told you, I have connections," he grinned secretively and truly, she didn't care. He was so thoughtful.

She felt a pang of guilt over her behavior the evening before. He'd been so nice to her from the beginning.

"Carson," she said as soon as she made it to the bed. "I owe you an apology. I know I joked earlier about being a dowdy, old maid, but I realized that last night I behaved like one. I'm sorry."

"I pushed you too much for a first date and I'm sorry. Truce?" he held out his hand to her, which she shook wholeheartedly.

"Truce!"

Her brilliant smile lit up the whole room. He had to hold himself back from gathering her in his arms and kissing her passionately.

"Now, when do you want to go out on my boat?"

Her face crumpled and she looked warily at the picture of Roger. "I don't know. Maybe when I feel better…"

He regretted bringing up what seemed to be a very serious topic for her, when his intention was the opposite. It was supposed to be about fun. "Are you afraid of the water?"

"No…at least I don't think so. I've never actually been on a boat before."

"Well then you're in for a treat! I have a feeling you're going to love it!"

She wasn't ready yet. She didn't want to do the one thing that Roger had asked of her. But she knew she owed it to him.

"How 'bout in two days?" That left her two days to heal her foot and to worry over the venture.

"Thursday, then?"

At her nod, he put his hands in his pockets and leaned casually against the wall. "Do you need anything else?" He tried to keep the desire out of his voice, but seeing her propped up in that huge, lush bed had his imagination doing overtime. God, how he wanted her.

"I – well, no, I don't think so."

He had to get out of there quickly. He wrote his cell phone number on a small slip of paper and left it by the phone. "If you need anything – and I mean anything, you call me on my cell phone and I'll be here in minutes, I promise."

Baffled by his continued kindness, but not wanting to look a gift horse in the mouth, she looked up at him. "Why are you doing this?"

"Doing what?"

"Being so nice to me? Especially after…well, after last night. Now that you know we're not going to…"

"Make love?" He was amused by the obvious discomfort the phrase made her feel.

"Uh, yes, I guess."

"Well, maybe I'm an optimist. And I can't stand to see a damsel in distress."

He leaned over her, his lips hovering tantalizingly near her lips, but he kissed her chastely on the forehead instead.

"Call me if you need me." And then he was gone.

Molly couldn't sleep again, most likely a result

of the nap she'd indulged in earlier. Something Carson said disturbed her…something about being an optimist.

Did he still think he could lure her into his bed? Of all the – well, she guessed it wasn't a complete impossibility and she was strangely flattered. She was still attracted to him, after all, but she didn't need a roaming, charming bachelor in her little world. He would hurt her; of that she was certain. A woman didn't love that man lightly and he would never love completely, so why risk it at all?

Be honest. Her conscious heeded.
He was so accurate in reading her desires, her fears. The idea of a passionate affair with a handsome rogue like Carson touched on a fantasy buried somewhere deep inside of her. He was wild, carefree, unable to stay in one place. He didn't want a commitment; he didn't need complications. He was a loner, free to go where he wanted, when he wanted.

Geez! She felt like she was writing an ad for the Marlboro Man! At least he was smart and responsible – he'd designed this hotel, hadn't he?

She was drawn to him inexplicably.

She considered what that meant. So what if there was nothing long-term in it for her? Couldn't she buck up and be a modern woman? Or was having an affair just too tawdry for her? It troubled her. This sparring back and forth in her head. Usually her good sense won out, but this time her body was on fire at the very thought of making love with him and it was going a long way towards over ruling her good sense.

Roger would tell her to throw caution to the wind and just sleep with the guy…well, actually his choice of words would be much more colorful, but the message would be the same. He'd often told her to let her hair down and live a little. The idea of a love affair in a tropical paradise would have made him proud and certainly not something *he* would have run from.

Molly thought of Carson's touch, imagining his large hands as they swept over her body. Heated sensations flowed through her, causing her to squirm in anticipatory wonder.

His kisses were such a clear memory, that her lips tingled as she recalled the passion she felt in his arms. Never before had a man made her feel both weak and powerful in a single action. He would possess her body fully, she knew, and demand her complete participation. Was she up for the challenge? Would she let him seduce her into his bed, but not into his heart?

Slipping into sleep at last, her final thought was that maybe, just maybe she would.

They were closing in on The Kid...he had to hide the merchandise. He was just supposed to be a messenger. Delivering discreet items to his customers...but this time, he had picked up something that was too hot. Too dangerous. He had to ditch it until he could get the heat off his back.

The little store at the "Shops at Waverly" was the perfect place. Dodging in to dispose of "the package" The Kid slipped past the two enormous Samoan thugs who were following him. He tucked the package toward the back of the display before picking up a Hawaiian shirt and a baseball cap. He paid for his items, donned them, and walked out the door.

He had a baby face and looked much younger than his age, often passing as a teenager. It served him well, because no one took a teenage boy seriously. But this was serious business. Very serious.

6

By noon the next day, Molly was feeling physically better, but bored out of her mind. She'd read through all the magazines and was halfway through one of the books Carson had brought her and she couldn't stand to be inside anymore.

The sand and sun was calling her, so she donned her bathing suit and made her way slowly to the pool. Her foot was significantly better today and she didn't require the cane. It was just as easy to prop her foot up on a lounge chair as it was a bed, she'd convinced herself, and was immediately happier.

The bar waitress was making her rounds, so Molly decided on a virgin mai tai and leaned back to surrender herself to the sun.

For the first time in over a week, she allowed herself to remember the final days with Roger. The doctors had given him the most potent painkillers they could give him, knowing that the Cancer had won and it was just a matter of time.

"Don't forget our promise, Mol," Roger

wheezed out as he grasped her hand with pitiful strength.

"I won't." The tears streamed down her face despite her attempt to hide them.

"Roger," she felt she had to tell him once again – just in case he had forgotten…"You are the best friend I've ever had. You changed my life. I love you, honey. I love you so much."

"I love you too, Mol. Go enjoy life. Get out there and find yourself a sexy, handsome man so I can smile down on you from heaven. You need to be a mother, Molly. You need a family. You. Need. Fun. Promise me."

"I promise." Her voice was broken with emotion. "I promise. Roger."

His eyes glazed over with pain as he breathed his last breath. "I'll say hi to God for you," he tried to smile just as he passed.

She would never forget that moment. His face suddenly became peaceful and she knew it was over.

A week later she sat in her cold apartment feeling lost and lonely. She hadn't slept in weeks and even though he was gone, sleep still eluded her. The urn holding his remains sat on her coffee table in front of the fireplace where they'd stay up late many nights talking about life and dreams.

Despite the many, many friends that Roger had made over the years, he had requested that there be no funeral. Only a simple memorial service with a few of his closest friends. All of the details were already arranged and she merely had to show up. Even that seemed like too much for Molly, but somehow she made it through.

She had one last mission, though she was

reluctant to carry it out. He'd wanted his ashes spread out in the ocean off the Poipu coast of Kauai.

Once, when he was a little boy, his family had gone to Kauai when his parents were still married. It had been the best summer of his life and his favorite memory was that of the day he spent snorkeling in that ocean with his father as his teacher. It wasn't long after that that his parents were divorced, leaving him sad and confused.

And later, as an adult, there was a disagreement that led to the destruction of his family's once cohesive unit. Gone was the comfort of having a solid, happy family life. So he wanted his memories, his life, preserved in the last place that he had felt true happiness.

It was such a shame, really, Molly thought now as she looked out at that very ocean, tears silently sliding down her cheeks. He was a brilliant and generous man – quite a successful entrepreneur.

In the mid-eighties he was a computer programmer for a company that soon became huge. His stock options made him a millionaire when the company went public and then he simply invested his money in high tech ventures.

She had nicknamed him "Midas", since everything he touched made him richer and richer.

He put money away for his parent's retirement, his niece and nephews college funds and bought his older sister a home in Connecticut. But his ghosts still haunted him, even toward the end. He tried to make peace with his family, but they were not as forgiving and understanding as he was. He, on the other hand, took care of them with the hopes that someday they would understand how much he loved them despite the bitter chasm in their relationship.

It infuriated Molly when she thought about it. None of them knew Roger like she did…how he loved to cook gourmet meals for friends…how he had a passion for Cribbage and Bingo…how he wrote dark, solemn poetry that he didn't think anyone should ever read…how he'd made her very dull, pathetic life come alive with excitement and love.

She tried not to hate his family, because even after all the pain they'd caused him, Roger did not hate them.

He told her once, "hate only hurts the hater. They suffer in their own ways and it's not for me to judge them, otherwise I would be no different."

She knew he was so right about that. Still, maybe someday she could think of them with the same kind of compassion in which Roger had. Someday.

Carson found Molly leaning back on the lounge chair, with her leg propped up on thick swimming towels. Her head tilted toward the sun as if she was saying to the Sun Goddess, "go ahead then, take me."

Tears wet her cheeks in long streams and he almost felt like he was violating her privacy. But he couldn't stay away. He took the mai tai from the waitress and gently laid it down on the small, round glass table beside Molly.

"It's on the house," he said softly and turned to walk away.

"Wait," Molly cried out to him to come back and motioned for him to take the chair next to her. "Can you stay a minute?"

"Of course," he had a meeting in less than a half hour, but he'd rather spend the rest of the afternoon with her. "Are you ok?"

He leaned over and wiped at the wetness on her cheeks. She nodded and reached for her sunglasses in hopes of belatedly hiding her grief.

"Would you like to talk about it? You look like you've just lost your best friend," he tried to sound funny, but at her wince, he instantly regretted it. "I'm so sorry, Molly."

"It's not your fault. I *did* just lose my best friend. My best friend of six years."

"Roger?" That would explain a lot to him. Was he her husband? Her lover? He had questions, but knew he had no right to ask.

"Yes." Her answer caught on a sob.

"Tell me," he encouraged her. What was it about this woman that made him want to slay dragons for her? Hmph. It was a foreign feeling for him and he didn't like it.

"I can't yet. It just happened a short time ago and I'm not ready yet. But thanks for asking."

Understanding her need to set the pace, he changed the subject. "How's the ankle?"

"Better," she managed a shaky smile. "I got down here without the cane."

"Good!" He seemed genuinely pleased for her.

"Carson," she was serious again as she reached out for his hand. He gave it to her.

"I want to thank you so much for all the things you've done for me. You've been a wonderful new…friend, and I'm so glad I met you."

Memories of Roger made her want to be at peace with people in her own life. She didn't want to die knowing that she could have said more…been more to people. He had taught her not to miss those precious opportunities.

"You're welcome, Molly." His smile was warm and kind. "I'm glad I met you too. My whole day brightens when I see you."

He was sincere, he realized, even though compliments to beautiful women usually flowed easily out of habit, whether he meant it or not. Thinking he needed to ponder that notion later, Carson again changed the subject. "Think you can make it on my boat tomorrow?"

She smiled. "Oh yes, of course…if you don't mind my wobbling around."

"I can take it if you can." The smile faded away and he stared at her with barely veiled intensity for a long moment.

His voice lowered, "How 'bout if I bring you dinner tonight? We can eat in your room."

She chewed on the inside of her lip, wondering if she should agree to something as intimate as dinner in her room. *Yes…please!* A voice insider her cried. Her body heated at the thought of another opportunity with this robust, handsome man. Would she chicken out again if given a second chance?

"I promise to be a perfect gentleman, though it will be very difficult to hold myself back from you." The smile in his eyes told her he was flirting with her, something she definitely wasn't used to.

"Well, ok. If you promise." And then, deciding to give him back a little, she took a deep breath before she teased, "but maybe I won't be a perfect gentlewoman."

He threw back his head and laughed, the sound sending warmth throughout her body. He had a sexy, low laugh that made her glad to be a woman at that very moment.

"I should be so lucky," he commented.

Leilani watched the exchange between her boss and Miss Carson. She was a little nervous that Molly would tell him about her awful behavior two nights ago. It had been grossly inappropriate of her to chastise a paying guest the way she had and she felt remorseful ever since.

Displaying an unusual amount of nervousness the past day, her father had taken her aside and simply said, "What have you done?"

It was unreal how well he knew his daughter's mischievous side and she ended up blurting out the whole scenario to him.

He shook his head in disappointment and merely said, "you need to make it right, Lei."

She nodded. This was her first opportunity to create an excuse to bump into Molly. As soon as Carson left, she took a deep breath and sat in the seat he deserted.

"Hello, Miss Carson," Leilani smiled nervously at Molly, who lowered her sunglasses to get a good look at her in daylight.

Quickly, she set her sunglasses back in place. It was better if she didn't see the woman's flawless beauty in broad daylight. She already felt grossly inadequate.

"Hello, Leilani," her voice was cool and distant. Molly had no desire to repeat the scene she experienced two nights before.

"I hope you're enjoying your stay," she began hesitantly.

Molly was not in the mood to beat around the bush, so she was uncharacteristically blunt. "How can I help you, Leilani?"

The young woman took a deep breath and tried for a sincere tone. "I owe you an apology for my behavior the other night. It was unprofessional of me and I'm very sorry."

Molly struggled to sit up and looked directly into the girl's eyes. She meant it, Molly could see, so she graciously said, "it's ok, Leilani. I was actually very surprised, but since I have no interest in Carson, it really shouldn't bother me, should it?" She smiled in appreciation of her little white lie.

"It's none of my business. Carson is a long time friend, Miss Carson. I've always had a little crush on him, but he has never shown any interest in me other than in a big brotherly way."

"Please don't call me Miss Carson. Goodness, it makes me feel ancient! Let's start again. I'm Molly."

They shook hands again as if for the first time.

"So how long have you known Carson?"

"Since I was fourteen. He worked with my father and I got to hang out during the whole summer that he was building the hotel. He kind of took me under his wing, like a – like a little sister, I guess."

Molly could imagine Carson being a sort of big brother to a young teenage girl, especially since he had practically raised his own brother and sisters.

Molly offered cautiously, "I'm sure he was very kind."

"He IS very kind and generous and understanding too. I wish he was my real brother." She sighed. "I don't have any siblings."

Her youthful admiration for him made Molly smile

"Miss Carson-"

"Molly," she corrected.

"Molly, I know you said you're not interested in Carson, but I thought you should know that I've never seen him act this way with another woman before." Intrigued in spite of herself, Molly tipped her glasses down again. The woman was telling the truth.

"Really?"

"Really. He'll sometimes have dinner an evening or two with someone, but I've never seen him pay such obvious attention to someone – a guest! - in broad daylight. I think he likes you."

Molly knew Leilani was just trying to make up for her behavior. She hated the glimmer of hope the woman's words inspired.

"Leilani, I'm not going to tell anyone about what happened. You don't need to make it up to me."

Leilani giggled. "You think I'm telling you these things so that you won't complain about me? Well, I'm not. I just thought you might like to know. That's it. No hidden agenda."

Molly didn't answer her for a long moment. It still surprised her that a man like Carson would show her more than a passing interest, especially if he was reputed to date models!

"It's just testosterone, Leilani," she said at last.

"What do you mean?"

"Well, he doesn't understand how someone simple like me could refuse his charm. He's challenged by me, that's all. It'll pass as soon as he becomes bored with me."

Her attempt to hide her disappointment was not successful. Leilani put a slender hand on Molly's petite one.

"I don't think so. He doesn't waste time with women who don't want him. It's not the kind of challenge that he enjoys. Besides, Carson is deeper than that."

"Either way, I'm not interested in a – a fling with someone, even Carson."

"You should be." The words came out sharper than she'd intended, so Leilani smiled to break the harshness. "I mean, he would be good for you. I couldn't help but notice that you were crying earlier. Is it a broken heart?"

Molly was not used to revealing her private emotions, but there was something sincerely kind in the way Leilani asked her, that she found herself answering honestly. "My best friend died a few weeks ago. He had cancer."

"Oh I'm so sorry!!!" Leilani gripped Molly's hand with fierce compassion and soon Molly had spilled the whole story with much more graphic detail than she'd had the opportunity to share with anyone.

Both had tears running down their faces when she was through.

Leilani dabbed at her eyes and said in a low voice, "Molly, you were such a good friend to him. I don't think I could have given everything up to nurse someone who was dying. I don't have it in me."

"He gave me the world, though, and I'm a better person for having been his friend. You probably could do it if you really loved someone. You never really know what your capable of until you are faced with a situation."

"Maybe," but she looked doubtful.

"I can't believe I told you all that. You're very easy to talk to!"

Molly sat up in her chair and eased her foot over the side. It was time for her to go in and take a shower. "And I feel better – really!"

"You're a good person, Molly. To nurse him the way you did and to fulfill his dying wishes. I hope I have a friend like you someday."

"Well, I guess sharing like this is a way of becoming friends, don't you think?"

Molly smiled at the young woman as she gathered her things. When she stood, they embraced lightly and went their separate ways.

Carson saw the exchange and wondered at the strange camaraderie between the two women.

When Leilani walked past him, he stopped her by touching her arm lightly. "What mischief are you up to now, Leilani?" His voice was low and menacing.

"Nothing, Carson. Just getting to know some of the guests," her smile was sweet, but he knew all to well that she could be deceptive.

It wouldn't be the first time she had tried to intercede in one of his associations. Despite the way he discouraged her romantically, she had a vicious jealous streak and paid far too much attention to his personal life.

"Lei.." he warned, but she waved him off.

"Molly is an amazing woman, Carson. Don't you hurt her." She took on a rarely admonishing tone, before continuing on to her office.

Carson stood looking after her, puzzled. Women!

Dinner was casually set on the balcony, which had an unobstructed view of the ocean. Carson had to wonder again how a nurse living in one of the most expensive cities in the US could afford one of his premium rooms. But it was none of his business, he reminded himself.

Carson directed the room-server on how he wanted the table set and then nodded his thanks, while Molly was busy taking her time in the bathroom. He looked around at her small suitcase and the few personal items that were not put away in either the drawers or the closet. She had the urn and the picture of her "friend"...Roger, sitting on the bedside table.

Curiously, he wondered again exactly what their relationship was. To bring his picture along on her vacation, well, it just seemed like he had to be more than a friend. A knife of jealously stabbed at his stomach, nearly sending him off his feet. He'd never been jealous a moment in his adult life until this woman came around! He did not like how it felt. In fact, he was overwhelmed with such distaste, that he took a sip of wine to try to banish it.

Still, he was unable to curb his curiosity, so he pried open the urn and found what appeared to be ashes. Two and two came together quickly as he put the urn back in it's original position. He felt like pond scum. Obviously, this was Roger. Her best friend. Her lover? Her husband?

Resisting the urge to hurl the urn across the room, Carson moved to the balcony. He was sipping his wine gazing out at the ocean when Molly came out. She wore a simple cotton sundress – different than the one she'd worn that first day. This one was a pale peach, which highlighted her recently sun-kissed skin and brown hair. She was exquisite in her petite simple grace.

Guilt swept over him again at the thought that he'd violated something that was clearly sacred to her.

She brought his ashes and his picture with her, for God's sake! As if they were on vacation together. He felt he understood her better now. Why she was so resistant to his advances. Why waves of pain shadowed her eyes when she thought he didn't notice. He did notice. And it tore at him. He wanted to soothe the pain away and make her forget. But she'd been with Roger for a long time – six years, she'd said. The horny scoundrel in him warred with the honor he seldom felt when it came to women. But Molly was different. He didn't understand it – could barely accept it, but she was different. And she didn't deserve to have a man like him pushing her to seduction. She deserved exactly what she'd called him earlier. A friend.

"You're beautiful, Molly," he said as he handed her a glass of wine.

"It's nice of you not to comment on my limping about…it's not exactly graceful." She had humor in her eyes and again he felt guilt. At least he could treat her respectfully for the rest of her trip.

"But you seem to be getting around better," he noted.

"Thanks to 500 milligrams of Advil!" It was true, she could put almost the regular pressure on her foot now and it didn't hurt like it did before. For that she was grateful.

Carson held the chair out for Molly and tucked her into the table. They sat the same way they had the night of their romantic dinner, so they could both see the ocean. The sun was just beginning to rest over the horizon, and long fingers of orange, pink, purple and gray made a startling canvas just above the dark ocean. Palm trees rustled in the wind and the air was thick with tropical humidity, now less pungent with the setting sun.

"This is nice." She felt more relaxed tonight. More like herself. It must be the sun, and the handsome company.

Glancing at Carson as he took a bite of his grilled Ahi, Molly once again noticed the lines of character around his eyes. There was compassion in his unusual eyes and kindness. It was difficult to reconcile this Carson with the one who was so obviously a player. He looked rugged and handsome and strong. His muscles were straining against the generously cut sleeves of his polo shirt.

He would be strong and aggressive in bed, but most likely gentle as well. It both frightened and exhilerated her. Months from now would she regret not taking advantage of this romantic situation he was so obviously handing her? She shook her head at the pity she felt that he was such a confirmed bachelor...a wanderer. If he hadn't been so open about it from the beginning, she might have actually fallen in love with him. The thought made her heart pound and her palms sweat. No, she mustn't think like that.

"Do I have parsley on my face?" He teased without even looking her way.

"What?"

"You keep staring at me like that and you're going to make me feel self-conscious. What is it?"

Blushing, Molly turned her attention to the Ahi with a pineapple sauce. "Nothing. I was just looking at your laugh lines. That's all."

"Great. Now you're probably thinking about how much older I am than you." He was teasing, but then he thought of Roger. Roger had to be at least 15 years her senior. Maybe she liked older men. The idea sobered his humor.

"Nah. I wasn't thinking about that. I was thinking how lucky you men are. Lines around your eyes are called laugh lines…for women, they're crows feet. It's just not fair."

He chuckled at her disgruntled sigh. For some reason she didn't seem like the type of woman who cared about aging. She just seemed too practical for that.

"So tell me," he pushed his empty plate away and leaned an elbow on the table. "What are your hopes and dreams, Molly?"

The question so took her by surprise, that she stopped eating and just stared at him. "What do you mean?"

"I mean…what do you want to do with your life? You're still pretty young, you know. What else do you see in your future?" *Now that Roger was dead.*

A flicker of amusement appeared on her face. "I thought you already knew me…"

He nearly choked on his wine, dreading another confrontation like the one two nights before. But he saw that she was only joking and he relaxed a little. "I have my thoughts, but I'd rather hear yours."

Her eyebrows knit in deep concentration as she fiddled with her fish. She hadn't thought about her own dreams in so long, that she had to dig deep to remember them. Marriage. A family of her own. Perhaps teaching children someday. They were all just simple dreams really, but they'd never seemed as unattainable as they did right now as she sat with this unavailable, eligible bachelor eating dinner overlooking the Pacific Ocean.

It seemed like years ago when she thought of herself as 'pretty young', and it disturbed her. When had she given up? A shiver ran through her and she physically shook at the thought. It was something she promised to give serious consideration. But for now that bachelor was staring intently at her, waiting for an answer. She wanted to sound impressive and come up with an exotic dream like hiking through the Himalayas or going on an African Safari, but the truth was, she had no interest in anything that foreign.

Truthfully, she answered. "I'd like to go to Italy someday. And maybe Spain." When he didn't comment, she continued. "I've always wanted to write a book – maybe a children's book. About going to the hospital or having family in the hospital. It's so hard for them, you know."

Still he just listened, and without meeting his eyes, she gazed out into the ocean.

"I could see you as a family woman. Maybe living in the country somewhere with your own home and property. A husband and lots of neighbors that you'd hang out with. You need babies, Molly." His gaze penetrated her concentration. He did seem to know her.

Looking away, she confirmed, "I always wanted a big family. Lot's of kids…but I prefer the beach to the country."

"Wanted?" he prompted. Roger was so obviously present this evening that Carson felt like he was violating some other guy's territory.

"Well, yes. I guess I'm thinking in the past tense. Things change." She looked so very sad then, that he had to resist taking her into his arms for comfort.

"You still have some time yet, you know." He smiled at her, willing her to relax again.

"I know. But it just seems like a far away dream now." She pulled herself out of her funk and attempted a smile. "Kind of like visiting the exotic island of Kauai!"

He smiled back and laid a hand on hers with companionable silence. "What other dreams, Molly?" he asked.

"You mean crazy 'out there' dreams?" He nodded. "I've always wanted to go up in a hot air balloon…or maybe even parachute, but I'm sure I'm too chicken to do that!"

He laughed at the idea of her jumping out of a plane, her crisp dress flapping around in the wind and her hair wild and tangled in her face. It was a stretch of the imagination.

"What about you? What are your dreams, Carson?" He liked the way she breathed out his name. It sounded husky and intimate when she said it.

"I've done a lot of the things I've wanted to do. I guess I don't believe in holding back."

"Like what?" She loved to hear about another person's adventures. She was the perfect vicarious armchair dreamer.

"Well, for starters, I've parachuted…in the dessert of Nevada. And I've done just about every sport you can imagine – sailing, golf, racquetball, basketball, skiing, snowboarding, cycling, football…just to name a few."

That would explain his fantastic body, she thought and then took a nervous sip of wine.

"I've also traveled all over the world."

"Where was your favorite place?" She asked leaning into him eagerly.

While he spoke she thought of her *Travel Magazine* hiding in the nightstand. Always before travel to exotic places had seemed so extravagant...so frivolous. But as she listened to his list of vacations, she realized it wasn't nearly as frivolous as she once thought. And now, more than ever, it was possible for her.

"Well, I've liked a lot of them...Your Italy and Spain...Costa Rica, Japan, Singapore, Australia. I didn't really like China or Russia."

"But your favorite," she prompted.

"I think I like San Francisco the best." He looked her directly in the eyes, wanting to see her reaction.

Blushing, she simply smiled. "You're just saying that."

"Why would I say that? It is my favorite city. It has the ocean, beautiful diverse neighborhoods, each with their own personality and great cultural features too."

"You said you have a home there...where is it?" It felt strange to be speaking of a common city here, in the beautiful serenity of Kauai.

"Not too far from North Beach, around the Waverly Hotel," he was specifically vague.

She sat up excitedly, "did you design that hotel also?"

He chuckled at her enthusiasm. "Yes, as a matter of fact, I did."

"I'm so impressed! You are very talented, Carson! The owners of the hotel must love your work!"

"Well, I suppose they think it's ok. They're

perfectionists and I just try to please." He smiled into his wine, enjoying his little game.

"But they've let you design two of their beautiful hotels and they are so exclusive!!" She felt as if she were in the presence of royalty. "I think I'm having dinner with a celebrity!"

She held her glass up to him, "to beautiful architectural creations by Carson…"she let the name drift off because she suddenly realized that she didn't know his last name. But it didn't matter. In fact, it was probably better that way.

He clinked her glass and drank and then held it up to her again.

"To far away dreams and hopes that they all come true."

She couldn't refuse his optimistic gesture and sipped again at her wine.

With a tilt of her head, she peered at him closely. "Have you ever been married?"

"Nope."

"In love?"

"Nope."

"What?! A man like you – I'm shocked!"

"Well, when I was a teenager I was in love with my Spanish teacher, Miss Gallegos, but that's about it."

"I don't understand. Why haven't you been in love before?"

He shifted in his seat, suddenly a little uncomfortable. "I told you – I'm not looking for commitments. I've cared deeply for someone before, but I can't say I've ever been in love."

Sighing, she put both elbows on the table and rested her chin on her folded hands. "Don't you believe in love?"

"No." He said it harshly, quickly – as if it were an instinctive response, one he didn't have to contemplate. "I mean – I believe in loving parents and siblings…even close friends. But actually being in love? No, I don't believe in it for me."

Sadness for Carson swept over Molly. She laid a gentle hand on his arm and felt, suddenly, like she was seeing Carson, the little boy. She wondered again at their conversation from several nights ago. Someone had hurt him deeply. Abandonment, perhaps, from his mother dying. He didn't meet her gaze but just took a sip of wine.

"Maybe you just haven't met her yet," she offered softly, wanting desperately to show the young person inside of him some sign of hope.

"Don't go there, Molly. Others have tried and it's no use." His tone warned her, but she didn't scare that easily.

Thinking of Roger and the painful past year, Molly could understand how someone would close their heart to love. She could almost feel it happening to her as he left her, but his life was every celebration of love, of acceptance, and she owed his memory to be open to loving again. The reward of love for however long it lasted, far outweighed the pain of loss.

"Carson, it will never happen if you constantly move around to avoid it. Maybe it's just a matter of staying in one place for a few moments."

Scraping back the chair and putting space between them, Carson walked to the balcony railing.

"I'm not interested in your psychological review of me, or in your pity." His anger was beginning to boil and somewhere outside of himself, he could look in and see that his reaction was much stronger than her compassion and guidance warranted. He didn't care. This subject was off limits.

"Ah. I see," she said quietly. "There you go again. Don't let anyone get too close. They might actually see you."

"It's none of your fucking business, Molly. Sometimes it's just that simple. I don't want to be with anyone, ok?"

He was angry. So angry. She realized that it was a clear indicator that she had hit somewhat close to home.

"There's no need to be vulgar. Fine. You prefer your own little prison. I'll leave it alone." She wasn't miffed, but she tilted her head in defiance anyway.

"It's not a prison. I wish you and every other Meddling Nellie would just get it through your heads. It's *your* gender's desire to settle down. I'm happy with the way things are, that's all. I don't have room in my life for marriage or a family. I just don't."

"Ok, ok. Whatever."

"Fine."

"Fine."

Molly went into the room and made herself busy with absolutely nothing.

Carson stood overlooking the ocean, willing himself to calm down. Why did he feel so angry? It was her eyes…those damned eyes. They were full of compassion for him and an understanding that he couldn't comprehend. And s*he* felt sorry for *him*! It was a joke. He had everything he wanted. She was the one walking around like a grieving widow! Why had the table suddenly turned? Damn women.

Finding some measure of control, Carson walked in to find Molly flipping channels on the TV.

"Are you done stewing?" she asked, not seeming the least bit perturbed. She was used to Roger's tantrums and didn't take it personally.

"I wasn't stewing…but yes, I'm done." He managed a weak smile.

She clicked off the TV and said, "then how 'bout a game of cards? I play a pretty mean game of Fish."

Laughing, he sat down at the table across from her and let her deal the cards. She was an amazing woman, he thought as she continued to surprise him with different aspects of her personality.

The kid paced back and forth in his small room at the rat-infested motel. He had not had a chance to retrieve the object from its hiding place because the area had been too hot. There were too many risks, but tomorrow, first thing in the morning, he would retrieve the package and deliver it to the boss. Or he'd find himself dead in a ditch somewhere.

7

The following morning, Molly got up early. She had a mission and she was determined to carry it out before Carson took her out in his boat. They were scheduled to leave the hotel at 11:00, so that only left her a few hours before he would come by her room.

Quickly, she showered and got made up. She arranged her beach bag with the urn, Roger's picture and her swimsuit before she set out to find Leilani – she needed the woman's help with her little secret project.

The main offices to the hotel were located along a special path that Carson had only pointed out during their tour. She hadn't actually been down the path, so she made her way until she saw a friendly receptionist sitting in the outdoor reception area. The office area was covered, but had no windows, allowing the gentle breeze to filter through along with the fresh air.

"Aloha. May I help you?" She was an older, Hawaiian woman and she wore the traditional mu-mu.

"Aloha – er, hi. I'm looking for Leilani…" She realized then that not only didn't she know Carson's last name, but she also didn't know her new friends. She made a mental note to learn it before she left.

"Why don't you have a seat –I'll ring her office."

"Mahalo. Thank you," Molly struggled to sound authentic, but her white skin and obvious tourist air gave her away. Thinking that not one person had made her feel like she didn't belong, she took one of the bamboo chairs lining the lobby. She loved the Aloha spirit!

"Molly!" Leilani glided unhurriedly toward her new friend and wrapped her in a warm embrace. "It's so nice to see you! Have you had breakfast? I was just going to take a break."

"Oh – thank you, but I've eaten. Actually, I'm in a little bit of a hurry and I'm hoping you can help me."

Leilani noticed the sparkle in Molly's eyes and sat down with her on the closest chair. "Of course! What do you need?"

Molly took a deep breath, "well, let me tell you what I have in mind."

A few moments later, Leilani walked Molly to the stone pathway that led to the "Shops at the Waverly" which was adjacent to the hotel, before leaving her to get back to work.

Smiling, she watched Molly proceed down the path. Carson was in bigger trouble than he bargained for, she thought. Molly was a great catch for him and she was going to do everything possible to help them along.

Her jealousy of Molly was no longer an issue,

especially since she'd met the young diver the previous evening at the Aloha Bar and Grill. Patrick. He was very charming and intelligent and she had immediately felt a connection. She was looking forward to the dinner he promised her for that evening. Sighing, she returned to her office. It was going to be a long day of daydreaming and waiting.

Molly found herself enjoying her little adventure, even if she was in a hurry to carry it out. It delighted her that every single foot of the hotel reflected island beauty, even this walk to the shops was filled with the green, lush shrubbery and trees lined the walk. The gentle, warm breeze transported the smell of fresh flowers and sea air. She nearly forgot for a moment that she was actually going shopping. It was a pleasant change from the city blocks she was accustomed to walking or the crowded malls with rows of chain stores. Once again, she appreciated Carson's preservation of the Hawaiian surroundings.

She found exactly what she was looking for at the fifth store she entered. It was a very nice, upscale souvenir shop that catered to an affluent clientele.

There was a section of island jewelry, which drew Molly's immediate attention. Among the racks of hibiscus necklaces and flip-flop charm bracelets, she found a rack of unique looking watches. They were certainly not cheap, but they were each designed a little bit differently. She picked up one that didn't have a tag and knew immediately that she had to have it. It had subtle designs of dolphin and little sparkles of sand set in the face of the watch. It was a diving watch and she could tell by its weight that it was well made.

"How much is this one?" she asked the clerk.

"Well, let's see. Oh, there's no tag. I'll ask the manager."

Molly was left to look at the other treasures locked in a glass case. She smiled at a teenage boy who stood nearby glancing through a worn comic book and blowing large bubbles with his gum. He glared at her and quickly looked away. She didn't take his response personally. Teenage boys were not exactly friendly with adults, she knew, and proceeded to view the jewelry on display.

Various earrings and necklaces made of shells, of rock and of carved wood covered the shelves. She had always been drawn to aquamarine and here, they had a lovely display of rings, bracelets and earrings. Perhaps one day she would indulge herself in a diamond and aquamarine ring, she thought. She could certainly afford it, but still, she hesitated. This little shopping venture was not about her.

"Two hundred fifty," the clerk returned with a tag in tow so that she could mark the watch.

"I'll take it," she said. It didn't really matter what it cost. She knew it was exactly the right thing.

The boy at the watch stand was watching Molly give her credit card to the clerk. He swore every word he could think of in his head, as the clerk wrapped the watch carefully for her. He'd blown it. He was supposed to get the watch back as soon as the heat died off, but even now the heat was on. He had come into the store with the intentions of retrieving the watch and hiding it in a more obscure place, but he was about two minutes too late.

Damn! His distaste over what he had to do settled in him with resignation. He didn't like violence — he was a courier for God's sake. But he was also reputed to get the job done no

matter what it took. Sometimes someone got in the way and he did what was necessary. He just hoped he wouldn't have to hurt anyone – especially a chick – in his effort to save his own ass.
Still, he had a job to do.

****

The first thing that Carson noticed about Molly when he picked her up at her room, was the glow of delight that warmed her cheeks. She looked like the cat had swallowed the canary! And he thought she'd never looked more beautiful. Stifling his body's response to her – for they were definitely only meant to be friends – he gave her a warm hug. It surprised her, leaving her flustered and speechless.

"Are you ready?" Carson asked, reaching for Molly's bag.

"I'll take that," she swooped in and grabbed the bag, quickly but carefully lifting it to her shoulder before he could quite reach it. "Yes, I'm ready!"

The drive to the dock was only a couple of miles. It was adjacent to the Waverly Golf Course, which was beautifully set on a grassy hill above the ocean. They drove in his Jeep Cherokee down to the dock, where even the dock master knew him.

"Ahoy, Carson!" He called through the open window of the car. Carson waved and proceeded to a parking place marked "reserved". When Molly raised an eyebrow in question, he merely grinned wickedly and said, "connections".

The "boat" was a forty five foot catamaran that took her breath away. It was completely white and had the words *"The Rogue"* painted on the side. It was very appropriate, she thought, letting a little laugh escape.

She oohed and ahhed as he assisted her on

board, instructing her to remove her street sandals first. His strong arms steadied her by holding her at the waist until she got her balance. He offered to take her bag, but she clutched it like a life support.

Shrugging, he untied the boat and started her up. Or was it a "him"? She wasn't versed in yacht-speak, but she decided it was a "she" after all.

Molly thought she'd never seen a more magnificent site than Carson at the helm of the boat, his brow furrowed in concentration as he took the vessel from the slip. It moved her. He was so natural here, so confident, she thought.

If only she could be that confident and self-assured. The only aspects of her life where she felt confident were in her nursing abilities and her friendship with Roger. But Roger was gone, she reminded herself.

Glancing around at the rest of the boat, she noticed stairs leading somewhere and asked him where they went.

"That leads to the main cabin and the head."

"What's a head?"

"The bathroom."

"Well, why don't they just call it a bathroom?" Rolling his eyes and smiling at the same time, he was amused by her practical logic.

"Do you want a life jacket?" He asked.

Whirling around, she met his gaze with wide-eyed alarm. "Do I need one?"

"Can you swim?"

"Of course."

"Then probably not."

She let out an exaggerated breath of relief, to which he laughed heartily in response.

Afraid to move around too much because the motion of the boat left her feeling unsteady and she didn't want to fall overboard, she cautiously sat on the front bench of the boat. Soon, the wind was whipping through her hair, and she forgot her fear as Carson brought *The Rogue* to full speed.

It was fabulous! She felt freer than she'd ever felt in her life. She felt both powerful and yet, so small when she considered the vast expanse of the open ocean. She breathed in the ocean air deeply, and closed her eyes as the waves crashed into the front of the boat. Feelings of anxiety and fear vanished as she allowed herself to sink into her newfound love of boats. It was absolute perfection.

Carson knew the moment the transition came for her as her head tilted back and her shoulders relaxed. The ocean always had the same affect on him and often he would come out alone and spend several days on the water as he detached from his responsibilities.

He wondered what she was thinking about as they headed south, in no particular direction. Pretty soon land seemed distant and obscure. There was only a small fishing boat barely discernable it was so far away. They were alone.

He turned off the engine and just let them drift for a time, so that he could join her.

More confident of her balance, she spontaneously jumped up on the bench where she was sitting and launched into his arms for a huge hug. He caught her easily and laughing, twirled her around. Laughing and exhilarated, she cried, "I love this – it's magnificent!!!!"

"I'm so glad. You seem born for the sea."

"Oh, I am! Now that I'm in my first boat, I know that I *was* born for it. You're right. I want to learn how to sail. I just decided right here and right now! When I get home I'll look into sailing lessons. OH! I'm so happy!"

He watched her glide over every inch of his boat, aware of the lump that had crept into his throat. He ached suddenly for all the sadness in her life. He doubted that she had said the words "I'm happy" very many times in her life. He felt regret for her. But just as quickly as his emotion came, it vanished; turned into satisfaction that he was able to make her exclaim such a thing. He wanted nothing more at that moment than to give her this kind of joy every single day that he was with her. The thought was so fleeting yet so strong, that he took a seat for a moment. It was a responsibility, he knew. One he took on as her new "friend". He refused to give it any other name.

"I'm glad you're happy, Molly. You deserve to be happy." He said it with deep sincerity in his voice as he rose and stood behind her. He wrapped a protective arm around her waist as they looked out into the vastness. It was his favorite solitary past time, one he used when he needed to get away by himself. For a change, he was glad to share it with Molly.

She hugged him to her side. "Thank you, Carson. You're so generous. I'm glad you're the one to take me here, on this journey."

"I'm glad you let me."

Teasing, she poked at him, "I'll bet all your women love this boat. It must be quite a tool in your seduction scheme!"

He looked first out to sea and then into her

eyes. "I've never brought a woman on board before."

"What? Why?" She didn't understand.

He shrugged and forced his tone to remain light, "it's my place. That's all."

Molly closed her mouth, which had dropped open in awe. She was momentarily speechless as she considered the great honor of being the first female on board.

"Carson-" she didn't know what to say, so she simply turned in his arms and squeezed him hard.

"Thank you," she said softly into his chest. Her response was simple but perfect, so Carson just nodded and rested his chin on the top of her head.

He thought it over since the previous night, and he realized that she'd come here for a purpose. He was going to help her if she'd let him.

After twenty or so minutes, she pulled away. He looked down into her eyes, and knew what she was thinking. It was time.

"I'm going to go bellow deck and- uh- do some stuff in the cabin. Holler if you need anything. Anything. Ok?"

He sensed that she had to be alone, though she didn't think he knew exactly why. She gripped his hand as he turned toward the stairs. "Thank you."

He nodded and disappeared below.

Gingerly, Molly took the urn from her bag and held it next to her bosom for a long embrace. She struggled to let go of the one person in her life who ever really mattered. Roger had known her inside and out. He saw the woman she was and encouraged the woman she could be. He was the only person in her life that had ever seen her so completely and he still loved her.

Despite months of preparation, she felt conflicted...between fulfilling a dying man's wish and truly letting go of her best friend. She knew she was being selfish to want to keep the urn full of his remains. It was something they had discussed – no argued over – more than once.

"I want you to move on, Molly," he had told her one night when they discussed his instructions. "I'll be in a place free of pain, honey, and I want that for you too. You need to let me go, so that you can live."

"I don't want to let you go, Rog," she tried desperately to hold back the tears that seemed to constantly be lodged in her throat. "I can't."

"Yes you can. You're stronger than you think you are." He held onto her hand as she laid her head on his chest. "My last year on this Earth would have been something dark and lonely and horrible if it hadn't been for you. Now I want to release you from the pain the same way that I'm being released from my pain. You'll know when it's time. But don't wait too long. I want to be free too, ok? I want to swim with the dolphins!"

She nodded, though there was still a protest that begged release from her. But how could she argue with his dying wishes? She kept the resistance in her heart at bay, trying with all her might to be brave for Roger.

Today, she felt his hand as if it were still in hers,

heard his voice in her head. "It's ok. It's time. Set me free, Molly," it seemed to say.

She clutched the urn close to her chest and held it there, her eyes closed tightly against the tears. "Oh Roger. I miss you so much. I'm so lonely without you," she whispered into the air, her little homily to her best friend. "You were such a great man. So brave. So generous. So smart. You taught me so much! You knew how to love without conditions and I learned how to love from you."

It felt right to say a few words…and she felt certain that he could hear her from wherever he was.

"Roger, you were so much fun to be with! You should have lived. You should have recovered from that horrible disease because you do so much good for the world. Sometimes I wish I could have taken your place. You mean more to the world, Roger. And the world needed you."

Brushing at her tears, she continued, lowering her voice as if she were confiding in him once again. "I wish you were still here with me, free of pain and disease. I just don't know what to do with my life now. I can't seem to get it together. I'm scared, Roger, so scared of being alone." She sobbed out a gut wrenching cry before twisting the lid off the urn.

"But you have to be set free – I know that. I love you, Roger. I will always love you with all of my heart. You will always be with me. Good-bye, my dear friend."

Holding carefully to the protective railing, she reached over the side of the boat and watched as the ashes cascaded out of the urn in a gentle swirl, mixing with the air, where it was freed into the wind. She saw it dust the sea, darkening it in places where it landed.

Other parts just drifted in the air as if looking for a comfortable place to land.

When the urn was empty, she carefully put the lid back on it, set it on the floor of the boat. "God bless you, Roger."

She finally let herself give in to the tears as she cried and cried.

She sobbed with her head leaning on her arm still stretched along the railing, her dangling hand open as if she were still trying to reach out to him, to keep him with her.

Carson let her have her space for more than a half hour. He paced back and forth in the small cabin, fighting with himself. She deserved her privacy, but every protective instinct within him, urged him to go to her and hold her.

He thought of her family and what little he knew about them. They lived several states away from her and he assumed that they'd probably never even met Roger.

Surely she had friends, but Roger had been her whole world - "her best friend". Molly seemed so very alone and her pain touched his heart. When he couldn't stand the sounds of her sobbing any longer, he went to her and sat beside her, gathering her into his lap.

"Shhhh." He said, gently running a strong hand up and down her back, along her brow and down her silky hair. "It's ok. You're not alone, Molly. I'm here. Go ahead and cry, honey."

He comforted her for what seemed to him like a long, long time as she sobbed and he tenderly rocked her back and forth. She muttered words he couldn't understand, her tears blazing heated wetness through his polo shirt. And still he held her.

It was late afternoon before either one of them moved. She quieted and, wiping her hand across her wet cheeks, she pulled away from him. She looked at him with surprise, as if she hadn't realized he was there, then bowed her head in embarrassment.

"Carson…" she didn't know what to say. She felt open and raw and vulnerable. How long had he held her? In his eyes, however, was a genuine, kind compassion.

He took and held her face in his hands and kissed her cheeks, her eyelids, her forehead. For someone who spent his life putting up walls, he seemed a natural at opening his heart to someone in need. She felt connected to him at a deep level now, something she'd never felt before, except with Roger.

It scared her. It seduced her.

"Shh, Molly. You don't have to say anything."

"But – I…"

"It's ok. You loved him. I know I say I don't believe in love, but I believe that you must have had a very special kind of love for this man. I'm so sorry for you that he's gone."

Feeling fresh tears sting her eyes, she nodded.

"He was lucky to have you, though. And if I know you at all, he'll always be in your heart and in your thoughts."

She nodded again, unable to speak just yet.

"Do you want to tell me about him?" He traced a finger along her hairline, moving a stray hair from her eyes. She looked up into his eyes, her blue gaze red from crying.

"I don't know if I can yet," her voice was gruff from her sobs, her mouth dry.

As if reading her mind, he offered, "Would you

like some water?"

He moved away at her nod and reached in the refrigerator for a bottle of water.

She accepted it from him with a weak smile of thanks as he assumed his position with her in his arms.

"How did you meet Roger?" He asked, prompting her. He personally knew about grieving and that it showed up in many different facets in life, not just death. He'd learned to be an expert too early in his own life.

She laughed weakly. "We lived in the same building when I first moved from Idaho. I was carrying in a box from my car and I bumped into him. He had a white poodle draped along one arm and a martini with a cigar in the other. His first words to me were, 'girl, you almost spilled my drink all over my new Jcrew shirt!' I apologized, but he waved it off. He said, 'first things first – put down that box.' He went to door #1 and rang the bell. A teenage boy answered and somehow, he managed to fish in his pocket for a fifty and said to the kid, 'unload this nice lady's car, will you?' And then he turned to me and said. 'I have another martini upstairs if you care to join me'. And we were inseparable after that."

Carson smiled. Roger sounded like one of the eccentric San Franciscans for which the city was known. He couldn't picture her with someone like that, but opposites sometimes attracted. She was smiling at the memory. He wanted more information from her. He wanted to know her, to understand this history that made her grieve so. The brief smile in memory made him more driven to take the pain away from her.

Talking, he knew, helped. "Tell me more…"

"Well, he was just about as crazy as I am

conservative, if you can believe that! He made it his personal challenge to get me to stretch my boundaries. Sometimes he won and sometimes he didn't."

"Like what?"

"Well, I was scared to death of the city when I first moved there. I wouldn't walk down the street unless I'd driven down it a hundred times and I wouldn't dream of using public transportation, even though it was more practical. Because of all the horror stories I'd heard about my whole life, I was afraid of getting mugged. Together we took a self-defense class, but I was still a big wimp. So, he invented a race. He bet me a week's salary that I couldn't ride bus 34 and 52 to the DeYoung Museum and back within two hours."

"What did you do?"

"Well, I bet him, of course – I love a good wager! And I won! I even had a half hour to look in on the Monet exhibit while I was there." She sat up proudly and was smiling at the memory. "The best part was that I got a week of HIS salary, which was five times mine. I paid off all my credit card bills with that bet!"

"How long have you known him?"

"Six years." Sighing, she leaned back into his arms. "This past year was the worst, though."

He didn't want her to go back to remembering all the pain she'd obviously been through, but he let her take the lead. It was her healing, after all.

"The cancer had gotten progressively worse even though they tried every known medical treatment and every alternative method. It was in his bones…his spine and his brain. There was nothing they could do, except control the pain."

"And you nursed him." He knew that Molly

Carson would love with her whole heart, body and soul. She was just that kind of woman. Once again he found himself thinking that Roger had been very lucky.

"Yes. I wish I could have done more," she admitted.

"I'm sure just being with him made him feel like the luckiest guy in the world."

"I hope so. He'd done so much for me – changed my life, really. I wanted to be there for him."

After several moments of silence, she laughed again. "He used to take me to gay bars and make me practice asking men or women to dance. I told him he was crazy – that a gay man would not dance with me. But he'd just scoff and say, 'and miss a chance to show their thing to all the hunters out there? Of course they'll dance with you. And they did. It was fun."

Carson stiffened as realization swept over him. The poodle. The martini. The gay bars. "He wasn't your husband?"

"Roger?" She practically shrieked in surprise. "Of course not!" She laughed heartily.

"Your lover? Your boyfriend?"

"Good Golly, no! He was as gay as they come, Carson! He was my best friend…my adopted big brother."

He didn't know what to do with the new information, but he suddenly felt a whole hell of a lot of relief. He'd been feeling guilty for hitting on a grieving widow and now he was absolved. He hugged her tighter. "I'm sorry, I guess I just assumed."

"Well," she was generous, "I could see why you'd think that way." She shivered as the late afternoon sun slipped past the hills of the closest island.

"We were inseparable and he was the closest

thing to a relationship that I've ever had."

Carson pondered her confession, allowing the jealousy he'd felt float out of his heart and into the wind. "Why, Molly?"

"Why what?" She turned in his arms to look at him.

"Why was he the closest thing to a relationship?"

Her delicate brows weaved together in a frown. "I just haven't had the opportunity, I guess."

He didn't buy it, so he persisted. "Why?"

"I'm not exactly beating off the men, Carson."

"You can't tell me that men don't approach you."

She shrugged her shoulders. "Not really, no."

"Maybe your 'vibe' puts them off."

Bristling a little, she cocked her head. "What 'vibe'?"

"The 'don't approach me' vibe."

"I don't know what you mean."

"Come on, Mol, I saw it from a mile away the first time I saw you." He rubbed her arms as if that would take the sting from his words.

She considered denying it, but was too tired to protest. She sank into his embrace with defeat.

"You're probably right."

"What are you afraid of, sweet?" His voice was gentle and little bit gruff as his body reacted to this new feeling of affection he had for her.

"Nothing…Everything. I don't know."

He kissed the top of her head and rocked her again. "Maybe you just need to practice with someone who is low risk."

He was thinking of himself, of course, and she

turned to look up at him with serious, wide, blue eyes.

Swallowing back her fear, she tried to sound bold, "maybe I do."

Warning signals were faint but they were there. H was anything but low risk. He was becoming more of a risk with every day that she saw him, learning about the many, complicated layers of which he was made.

He kissed the tip of her nose and then gently her lips for a brief, meaningful moment.

"I should get you back," he said, his voice gruff with sudden emotion. He wanted to apologize to her again, but for what he didn't know. Perhaps it was because he wasn't the man that she needed. Perhaps because he could never give her anything more a few pleasurable nights in his arms and maybe an occasional visit when he was in her city. She deserved more…so much more. He regretted it. More than he wanted to admit.

"Yes, I suppose." She turned to him then and held his hands in hers. It was a funny sight…her small, pale hands holding his large, dark ones. "But before we go, I want to give you something."

Fishing in her bag, she came up with a wrapped box. Handing it to him proudly, she announced, "this is for you."

He couldn't have been more surprised – his mouth actually fell open. "What is it?"

He reminded her of a little boy with wide-eyed awe and, she thought, just a little skepticism. "Well, open it, silly."

"Why?"

She rolled her eyes. "So you can see what's in it…" At his hesitation and deep frown, she blinked in alarm. "What's wrong? Haven't you ever gotten a present before?"

Carson flashed on one Christmas with his new stepmother. She'd taken a liking to the other children because they were so much younger than he and he was nothing but an independent, rebellious teenager of seventeen. She had various packages under the tree for the others, but when his little brother asked where Carson's gifts were, she threw a hateful look his way. "He doesn't get anything," she snapped. His father, of course, was away on business.

"Very rarely," he admitted. He was the one who showered gifts on people, because it was easier…stronger to be the giver. Seldom was he the recipient, which had been fine with him, until now. He was almost afraid to open the small package. "But why did you do this?" He just didn't understand.

She sat down next to him again and looked him right in the eyes. "Because there's only one other person in my life who has ever shown me the kind of kindness you've shown me the past few days. It gives me hope that people like you and Roger exist out in this crazy world. So, I want to thank you. It's nothing but a little token, really."

Carefully, he peeled off the wrapping paper and opened the box. When he saw the watch, he examined it very closely. It was a high end diving watch, with the ability to light while under water and track the depth in which he was diving. It was large enough for his big wrist and the dial was easy to read. It was perfect for him.

His silence made her uneasy and the rambling began. "It's a diving watch – I have no idea if you dive, but it seemed like it suited you. You said you liked sports and with Kauai being your home part time, I figured you could always use a diving watch…especially on the boat…But if you don't like it, we can return it-"

It suited him more than he could express to her. "It's perfect, Molly. You didn't have to do this."

"I wanted to."

"But it's expensive and really unnecessary."

"I think the appropriate response when someone gives you a gift, is to say 'thank you'."

"Thank you, Molly, very, very much." He was touched. So very touched that he didn't know what else to do, but to lean over and kiss her gently on the lips. When he pulled away, he noticed the color that rushed to her cheeks as she tried to look away.

"Will you hold onto it until we get back to land?"

"Of course." She tucked the watch back in her bag. "Now. Can we please head back? I'm freezing!!!!" She hugged her windbreaker close to her and pretended to shiver. And they were off.

"Do you want to drive?"

At her wide eyes, he threw back his head with laughter. He felt lighter, happier than he had in a long time. "Come on," he said taking her hand and dragging her to the large wheel as he started up the engine. "I'll show you how."

"But what if we crash?" She trembled with fear, but also with excited anticipation. Oh yes, she wanted to drive this beautiful craft!

"We're in the middle of the damned ocean – we're not going to crash!"

When she looked doubtfully at him, he pushed her in front of him at the wheel and allowed her to get accustomed to the feel of it.

Her back was to his strong chest and she felt

secure with the strong protective shell of his body. He also provided warmth and the rumble of his encouraging words gave her strength.

"Here," he said as he was letting go and giving her control. "Take it."

"But which way…? How do I…? What am I doing?"

He put two hands on her shoulders and whispered into her ear, "trust me. Trust yourself."

She did and soon she was driving completely on her own, unaware the Carson had moved to a seat behind her, watching her as her hair flew behind her and her feet parted to provide balance as she crashed through the ocean.

She looked exceptionally beautiful. Free of the pain she had been feeling and in a completely new element. He was happy just watching her. Happy being with her. He couldn't take his eyes off her even when she tossed her head his way and hollered, "you sneaky devil!"

He laughed and patted her affectionately on her bottom.

"You're doing great," he shouted back.

The kid lowered the binoculars he had taken with him on the fishing boat he borrowed from an associate. So, she'd given him the watch, he thought to himself. He snarled at their stupid, little romantic love fest. The woman had poured something over the side of the catamaran, though he didn't know what, nor did he care. All he cared about was the watch, which she finally produced as a gift to that asshole.

His hours of diligent watching had finally paid off. Retrieving it would be easy enough. He'd have it back by tonight and finally get paid for his troubles.

8

Molly declined Carson's offer for dinner that night. She was exhausted from their adventure and still a little sad about saying good-bye to Roger.

Two hours later, however, as she sat on the balcony, restless and unable to feel content in her own company, Molly felt empty. Her long shower had washed the remaining grief from her heart, so that all that remained was a desolate, lonely feeling. She missed Roger, but more, she felt as if she had just been introduced to her true self. Letting go of Roger had given her the space to open up to the possibilities that her new life now offered her. There were no more excuses for not moving forward with her life.

It scared her; it excited her. And despite it all, tonight she felt unsure of herself and even a little lost.

Grabbing a sweater, Molly closed the door behind her and headed to the elevators. She felt the ocean calling her and she decided that a walk on its shore would help clear her head.

She passed the social ruckus at the The Dock and took the stone pathway that led to the sand. Once there, she took off her sandals and rolled her white cotton pants up. Suddenly the need to feel the water on her feet was overpowering and she hobble-ran, leaving her sweater and her sandals on a hammock.

The shock of the cool water had her squealing and turning back to the dryer sand, but only for a moment. She knew she just needed to get accustomed to its temperature. A few daring attempts later and she had success. She walked the long beach with her feet in the water, looking at the moonlit horizon. It was so beautiful here. So serene and so far away from the problems in her life. It was exactly the therapy she needed.

Carson watched Molly as she disappeared into the night, the glow of the hotel lights losing her as she walk-ran along the surf. He was reluctant to invade her private thoughts, but when he saw her sneak past the bar, he followed her here, and watched her venture into the water.

He didn't like the fact that he thought about her. A lot. It reminded him of a craving, an obsession and he didn't like it at all. Still, he was intrigued and drawn to her now as she toyed with the water the way she was unknowingly toying with him.

He knew exactly what she was doing and he approved. She was thinking and grieving and letting the water cleanse her. Her love and friendship for Roger was no different than he had with his lifetime, best friend, Bob, he supposed. She seemed fiercely loyal to him, another thing he could relate to. He may not stay in one place very long, but he was loyal and dependable, especially when someone he loved needed him.

She was part of his inner circle now, there was no denying it. He didn't exactly love her, but he felt a responsibility to her after what they'd shared.

Thoughtfully, he wondered how he might feel when she left the island – and his life – when her vacation was over. Never before had he given anything other than a casual thought to the people he met while they were on vacation. It was just the way it was.

Carson was accustomed to short, hot romances that lasted about a week at a time. Sometimes two weeks if the woman was really something.

But she was different – this situation was different and the idea of never talking to her again troubled him. He wanted to see how she fared now that Roger was dead. He wanted to know her better.

He really cared about Molly Carson, he realized. He didn't want to care, but God help him, he did. He felt close to her and he was drawn to her in a way he had never been drawn to a woman. The innocence and purity at one moment and then heat from her sexual response to his kisses the next. His attraction to her was potent and instead of wearing thin as it usually did, after a few days, it was growing stronger. Deeper.

More of a concern, however, was that he was not just drawn to her physically, but he was attracted to her loyalty, her compassion, her love. She was interesting and fun to talk to. He was also attracted to something that he couldn't put his finder on. Perhaps it was her potential, he thought. She'd reached a crossroads in her life and he was could feel her conflicted wonderings about her future.

Perhaps that's what she was pondering along the beach tonight. She'd quit her job to take care of Roger and now she wasn't sure what to do with her life.

She needed a home and a good man and babies – lots of babies.

Carson shook his head. Since when did he think about babies? For crying out loud. His annoyance at himself had him returning to the bar for another Corona. He just needed to remind himself of the great life he had and forget about his little nurse's problems for a few hours.

Molly found a large log, stranded on the beach about a mile into her walk. It was perfect, she thought. Curling her legs up into an Indian style position, she sat, facing the ocean and thinking about her future.

Thanks to Roger, she would never have to worry about money again. The idea was both exciting and sobering. It opened a whole world up to her and she was scared witless. The question that Carson had asked her about her hopes and dreams niggled at the back of her mind, and now she gave it room to flourish.

Wouldn't this be the time to pursue some of those hopes and dreams? The idea of conservative, shy Molly Carson travelling the world almost made her laugh out loud. But a part of her yearned for exactly that kind of adventure. It seemed that now the whole world was opened up to her. The idea was boundless and vast.

Maybe it was time for her to redefine herself. Roger had always said she had much inside of her that she should show the world…and yet she had always just seen herself as a young woman from Idaho doing good work at St. Mary's. It was easier that way. Simpler.

She'd once thought she had had her life adventure when she moved to San Francisco. But now she was not sure that would be enough to sustain her throughout life. This yearning for more had taken on a life of it's own, in the form of a faint ache in her soul.

The moon, high in the sky now, reflected the dark patterns of the water. The gentle waves that crashed in a seaside rhythm were soothing.

Finally she was able to take a deep breath and acknowledge what was really tormenting her. A deep, foreign desire which seemed to roll throughout her gut, was at the heart of her turmoil.

Carson had awakened something inside of her that she had stuffed for a long time…her passion. Ever since he'd kissed her by the waterfall, she felt herself in a constant state of anxious anticipation. Her body was suddenly alive and thirsting for more – more passion – more touching – more Carson.

In the days since that first kiss, he had shown her small evidence of his true nature. He was kind, funny and intelligent. He was generous but humble and yes, he was somewhat arrogant. He had clear boundaries of what he was willing to share of himself and what was off limits. Grudgingly, she respected that. His will would cause him to put limitations on the level of intimacy that he shared with any woman and if that woman didn't respect that, then he would walk away without a backward glance.

Molly was beginning to accept his carefully guarded affection, though it made her sad that their friendship would hold such limitations. She wanted to free him of his darkness the way that he helped free her during her time of grief. But he wouldn't allow it and she felt such disappointment that a single small tear escaped her eye to travel down her cheek. There were "if onlys" and "what ifs", but the truth was that she should just accept him as he was or she would only push him away. And his friendship – in whatever form it took - was something she wanted to cling to now especially since Roger was gone.

It was not wise to want a man like Carson, she knew. His boat was aptly named after him. *The Rogue*. That's exactly what he was. A rogue who didn't believe in love.

There was no denying that his touch had made her hunger for physical release in a way she had never known. Oh, she'd had boyfriends in high school and even a few dates in college. But after that one incident in her dorm room when her virginity was taken – not given, but taken – she had stayed away from men in general. It seemed so long ago.

The long ago terror of that evening hardly mattered any more, now that she had tasted Carson's kisses. She was not afraid of him. She wanted him. But could she satisfy herself with a meaningless affair with her rogue? She wanted to try…oh how she wanted to try.

Maybe she should look at it as part of the process of redefining herself. If she could have an affair with him and then move on in her life, she would be crossing an invisible line of her own womanhood. Perhaps then she would be ready to date someone and settle down. After her travels, of course.

The idea appealed to her so much, that she almost fell off the log in her attempt to get up and go to him. She had to find him before she lost her courage. Excited for the first time in many years, Molly brushed at her pants. She hop-skipped even with her sore ankle, along the water and silently thanked God for the beauty of this place.

She wanted to find Carson before she lost her nerve.

Carson saw Molly return and couldn't hold himself back from descending on her as she sat in the hammock and strapped on her sandals.

"I was worried about you," he said, his voice low and gruff. It was true and it pissed him off that he was worried.

She'd been gone – out of his sight for almost two hours. He'd given her two more minutes before he would set after her, when she appeared in his line of sight, a dark figure splashing in the ocean.

Molly looked up at him as he stood several feet away, his hands on his hips. He'd startled her and her heart was beating ferociously.

She looked different – stronger. Her usually perfect hair was wild from the wind and she had a look of intent that had his mouth watering. God, he wanted her.

Without a word, Molly stood from the hammock and went to him. She reached a hand up to his neck and stood on tiptoe, her body pressing into his as she pulled him down to her. She kissed him like she hadn't kissed him before. It was on her terms. Her decision.

His anger vanished and turned into raw heat in an instant. Carson felt his head spin as she leaned into him and pulled him into her. It was akin to what it might feel like to drown, for most surely he was drowning in her newly confident kiss, her taste, her touch. He felt himself coming closer to that turning point where he wouldn't be able to stop himself and he had to pull back.

It was a struggle to pull his lips away from hers, but if he had any hope at all of keeping his head, this was the time in which to do it.

"Molly." His voice was low and rough and tortured. He held her head, her hair tangled in his hands as he cupped her face. "Molly, you're killing me. Please." Please what? Please let me ravage you here on the beach? Please stop before I do…what?!

But her eyes were clear and she looked intent. "Let's go," she whispered, her voice just as gruff as his with passion. She took him by the hand and together they passed the bar and through the lobby to the elevators.

Carson either ignored or didn't see the grins and nods in his direction from Sam and Leilani, because he couldn't take his eyes off of Molly. She had changed, he thought. She had clearly turned a corner and seemed to know exactly what she was doing. But what she was doing exactly, he didn't know. He had to know. For once in his adult life, he didn't want this to be a meaningless fling that they would both regret. She was more to him – how much more, he had no idea.

He had to clear up a few things before he took her – and he would take her and make love to her like he'd never done with a woman before. He didn't know what he really felt or what it all meant, he just knew it mattered.

"Molly," he breathed when they were on the elevator. "Talk to me, honey."

"I'd rather do this," she practically crawled up his body and attacked his mouth again. She couldn't get enough of him. The taste of him, his touch, his voice…it all consumed her and for once in her life, she didn't want to think at all. She wanted to lose herself in him – to Hell with all that was practical!

He held her up against him, she was so light in his arms, her legs straddling his waist. There they could both feel the evidence of his desire for her.

"Oh God," he moaned as she wiggled against him. When the elevator dinged at the appropriate floor, she slid seductively down his body, nearly sending him into a convulsion. Her eyes were wide with concern when he winced and nearly bent over.

"Carson?" For a moment, the alarm she felt outweighed her desire. But just for a moment. He let out a strained laugh and even that sounded sexy to her.

"It's ok, Molly. Do you have your key?" He took it from her and they practically ran from the elevator to her door, never leaving each other's arms.

She chewed on her inner lip as she watched him with the lock. For a single moment, she wavered.

Feeling her hesitation, he turned to her and looked directly into her blue eyes.

"Are you sure?"

It was a question. It was a warning. At her nod, he turned the handle and they were in, tumbling toward the bed in the dark.

Together, they crashed onto the large bed and tore at each other, their outer clothes easily and quickly discarded.

"Wait," he said, reaching for the lamp beside the bed. She froze.

Why was he stopping? He changed his mind, she decided. It was too good to be true.

"I want to see you," he practically growled.

Her disappointment quickly turned to self-consciousness as she tried to cover herself.

He was amused by her modesty and not at all surprised. He moved first one, then the other hand away to hold them above her head with one hand, and found himself looking at a very practical, white cotton bra.

What he hadn't expected – hadn't even really appreciated when she'd been in her conservative swimsuit, were her full, generous breasts. It almost startled him, but his body took over, and soon the bra was removed and lying on the floor somewhere across the room.

"Ah, Molly. You have beautiful breasts."

He proved it to her, by gently caressing first one, then the other. He didn't grab. He didn't squeeze. He just touched her with a feather light caress. Her nipples responded immediately and she arched her back, bringing her up closer to him. He accepted the invitation, his mouth descending to taste her. She cried out with pleasure as his mouth tickled and tasted and tortured her.

She held fast to his head, keeping his mouth exactly where it was. It felt like nothing she'd ever experienced before – her whole body was on fire like she'd never known. It was confusing and glorious and amazing.

Even as she lay there with him halfway on top of her, she could feel his arousal against her leg. Her heart beat wildly in her chest. She was scared. She was excited. She was ready for him.

"Carson, please," she breathed.

In one move, which left her feeling cool awareness of her body, he stood and removed his shorts – he wore nothing underneath them. She felt her mouth drop open as she stared – she couldn't help but stare – at his hard strength before her. It loomed, powerful and menacing, in front of her face and she didn't know what to do. So she did what came as a natural response…she reached for it with her small hand and brought it to her mouth.

"Jesus, Molly," he groaned and scooped up her curls to keep them out of her face. He wanted to watch her – God, how she looked stunning in her virgin-like amazement. But he knew that if she continued along that path, their first time would end too quickly and they would both be disappointed.

"Honey, stop," he said, and when she looked at him with worried eyes, he joined her on the bed and brought her close.

"No worries, ok? I just don't want to come too quickly. You're making me crazy."

Delighted and a little embarrassed that she could have such power, Molly nodded with a grin.

"You, on the other hand," he said with a growl as he tore at her white cotton panties, "can come as much as you want."

She had heard of orgasm – for crying out loud, she hadn't lived in a cave! But when his rough, thick fingers found her moistness and drove her, she felt herself falling, falling – or was it flying? Yes, flying into lights that seemed to spin a kaleidoscope in her head.

"Carson – "She cried out as her body arched in response, her head twisting this way and that as she thought for certain she'd found heaven. Everything in her shook as she climaxed under his talented fingers.

He watched her gloriously abandon herself to the moment and wanted a million moments just like this with her.

When her first climax died down, she lay

shaking in his arms, close to tears.

"Carson," she whispered again as he held her.

He lovingly kissed her forehead, her cheeks, her nose and finally, her mouth. Despite the agony of wanting his own release, he felt concerned over her soft sob.

He could feel her emotion and it touched him. God, he didn't want to admit how very much she touched his heart.

"Are you ok, darling?"

She nodded and looked him directly in the eyes. His kindness and concern for her only fed her growing passion. Her body still ached from a need only he could fulfill.

"I want you inside of me," she breathed huskily, which elicited another growl from him.

Still, he held himself back for a moment longer.

"Molly – I…" He didn't know what to say. How could he tell her what he was feeling when he barely understood it himself? That she wasn't just another one of his women? He wanted to be inside her more than he'd ever wanted anything in his life and that scared the shit out of him. But he had no promises to make. No words of love to be uttered. And still the questions surfaced in his head. He had to know.

"Molly, why?"

She looked doubtful and unsure of herself. He wanted to reassure her – but for now, he was the one who needed reassurance.

"Because – I…" She tried to recreate the thoughts she'd experienced while on the beach. It had made sense then but now it eluded her.

Then, she saw something in his eyes that gave her courage. She saw his doubt, his level of vulnerability and that was enough for her to shelve her own.

"Because, Carson. I've never felt this way before. I trust you."

Seeing the doubt war with something else that she couldn't read, she reassured him.

"Don't worry – I know what I'm doing." She put a small hand to his broad chin and looked directly in his eyes. "I don't have any expectations of you – just this…our special friendship or whatever it is at this moment, ok?"

Doubt was replaced with smoldering desire, the effect she was hoping for.

With a funny she-growl, she added "And you are the most sexy man I've ever met. If you don't hurry up – I'm going to scream!"

"Oh you're going to scream alright." He teased.

He positioned himself over her with a growl-chuckle combination, gently wrapping her legs around him. She was very tight and he was very big. He didn't want to hurt her, but his body had another, more urgent notion. To get inside. She was warm and wet and his instinct couldn't be stopped now. With one thrust, he entered her and felt her whole body go tense at the invasion as she gasped in discomfort.

"Shhhhh," he said when she was about to say something. "Just relax. It will take a minute for you to get used to me. It's ok, sweet. It's ok."

He whispered words of encouragement against her lips and after several moments, she began to move.

Her body also had a mind of its own. Once the initial discomfort faded, she felt heated and alive once again. She felt giddy at the idea that he was so deeply inside of her. It was raw, passionate pleasure that she felt now.

Greedy from her first climax, she wanted another. And she wanted him to have one as well.

"Oh God, Molly."

She was moving against him, bringing him into the motion with her hips and her legs pressed against him as she lifted herself to receive more of him. He had no choice, really, but to delve deeper. And he did.

"Carson," she whispered as the kiss she planted on his shoulder turned into a gentle bite, her nails digging into his broad back. Her body was alive with sensations she had no idea she could have.

"You feel – so-" she gasped as he thrust again, "g-good inside me."

He kissed her head, willing his body to slow down so she could peak again. "God, you're so sweet, so tight. Your body was made for mine, Molly."

She cried out as he reached between their bodies and found her most sensitive, swollen nub.

"Come on, sweet," he urged, his voice gruff and demanding in her ear. "Come to me."

Her body responded with more shooting stars, sending her into orgasm once again as she clutched at his broad shoulders and cried out his name.

He couldn't hold back any longer. With stroke after stroke, he too called out as his whole body shook in completion. He collapsed on her, half aware that he could be crushing her with the weight of his body. For a moment, he didn't give a damn.

He rolled to the side and gathered her in his arms.

She had watched his face when he came and felt a female pride that she didn't know she could feel. He was so complex, this big, handsome man of hers.

Witnessing his strength and power and vulnerability all at once moved her. It was primitive and elemental and something she didn't quite understand.

He propped himself up on an elbow, gazing at her body as his hand traveled up and down her.

"Molly, you're very beautiful," he said, his voice soft and gentle.

She blushed at the compliment. He was really the first man to see her completely naked and she felt that any response would seem inadequately inept. Pillow talk – however fanciful it was – was not her strength.

Her silence intrigued him. "You *do* know you're beautiful, don't you?"

At her modest shake of the head, he continued.

"How could you not? Surely men have told you this before?"

She looked away from him, feeling shame at her lack of experience.

"Molly?" He wasn't going to let this be, because he could feel its importance as his question dangled in the air.

"Carson…I haven't exactly been with very many men before."

"Well, I know that. But with enough to tell you how beautiful you are, right?"

"No. You're the first."

"The first…?" He felt panic rising in his chest. Had he just taken a virgin?

"The first to see me naked."

"What? I don't understand…are – were you a virgin?"

He had never been with a virgin before and her

body's resistance was certainly obvious, but he thought it was just because of his size. Women had mentioned it before, but in this case, he would not be surprised at all to find her complete innocence.

"Not really." She was having difficulty finding a good explanation and she wouldn't look him directly in the eyes. She began to fidget, a sure sign that something was not as it seemed.

"What do you mean, not really? Either you were or you weren't" His voice was raised and he couldn't stop the anger he was beginning to feel.

"I wasn't," she was beginning to feel anger too. He was grilling her and she just wanted to fall sleep in his arms. She was tired and sated, her body more relaxed than it had ever been. But she could tell that he wasn't going to let it pass.

"There was one guy – in college. He – well, he…"

His gaze pinned her to the pillow with its intensity even as his body leaned over her threateningly.

"He what?" he growled.

"He didn't take the time to undress me. He just sort of…you know."

"Tell me." It was a command.

She hadn't thought of 'the incident' in many years. It had lost its importance in her life. To be pulled back to the horror of that time was not something she wanted to do. "Carson, please."

"Molly."

She turned her head and clamped her eyes shut as she blurted out an abbreviated version of the story. How her roommate's boyfriend had snuck into their dorm room one night when her roommate had gone home for the weekend and clamped a hand over her mouth…At least it had been quick she later reconciled with herself.

She could feel Carson's body tense up and she didn't dare look at him. She felt ashamed and hideously naked at what she had just revealed. She had only ever told one person about the ordeal – Roger – and he had cried with her, just like a girlfriend would have. She didn't think the memory had any more power over her, but she was wrong. Little steps, she told herself.

One tear slipped out of her closed eyes and onto the pillow. She hoped he didn't see.

Several seconds passed as Carson took several deep breaths to calm himself. He wanted to murder that son of a bitch college kid, though he knew this wasn't about what he wanted right now. He felt like a shmuck for forcing her to tell her story when she clearly didn't want to.

Gently, he reached out and took her chin in his hand and turned her head toward him.

"Molly, open your eyes." His voice had lost the anger and he tried to focus on keeping it under control.

"Molly," he whispered.

She squinted at him with one eye, unsure of what she would find. Since he didn't look like he was going to blow a gasket, she opened her eyes. They were misty with unshed tears.

"I'm sorry, Molly." He said it with such sincerity, that the lump that had crept into her throat grew. She couldn't speak, so she merely shook her head at him.

"I'm sorry that it happened to you and I'm sorry I made you tell me. I had no right."

She realized then that he wasn't feeling pity or disappointment at her. He was genuinely sorry.

"It's ok," she said at last, her voice gruff with emotion.

"And there's been no one since?" She had already alluded to that fact, but he found that he needed it spelled out distinctly to unravel the curl of tension in his gut.

She shook her head.

"I'm so sorry," he said again, raining gentle kisses on her face.

He smiled slightly. "But I'm not sorry that I was the one you decided to share yourself with after all these years. It means something to me, Molly."

It meant something to her too, she thought. More than she was willing to admit. She was treading a very fine line with the safety of her heart and they both knew it.

"It was wonderful," she smiled brilliantly back at him, remembering their passion of only a few minutes prior.

"It was." His eyes took on the smoky glaze of desire again and she felt movement at her thigh.

Her eyes opened wide when he said, "I'll be able to go longer this time." His mouth descended on her again.

9

Carson regretted having to leave Molly when the sun came up. They'd spent every hour of the dark night talking, making love and laughing together. It had been the best night of his life. Instead of feeling exhausted, as he should, he felt energized and wanted to make love to her again. But she slept softly, her hair spread wildly on the pillow and over her face. She was incredible on so many levels.

He left her a note telling her he had to go to work, but that he would find her during the day sometime. He kissed her gently on the forehead and took one, last inhale of her scent before he rose and headed toward the door. His body knew the scent well and – amazingly – responded once again.

He was able to make it to his penthouse suite without being seen, which was good for Molly's sake. He didn't really care about his reputation, but he didn't want anyone thinking negatively about her.

As he approached the door to his suite, all thoughts of Molly drained from his mind. His door was open slightly. He kicked it open the rest of the way and did a quick search of his rooms. They had been tossed – and not very neatly, he discovered. Clothes were dripping out of the drawers, onto the floor, his bed was torn apart, his desk completely upended.

Every drawer and cupboard had been searched – for what, though, he hadn't a clue. He called his head of security and within three minutes there was a whole team in his suite.

They began taking fingerprints, but for some reason, Carson had a feeling they wouldn't find any. The guy may have been hasty, but he was most likely professional to have gotten past the keypad alarm to his floor and into his suite.

"Are you missing anything, boss?" Harvey, the head of security had his notepad out as he interviewed Carson.

"Some cash I had lying on my dresser. A couple of gold cufflinks. But that's it. He didn't take anything from my safe."

The burglar had not been interested in his laptop or digital camera. It was almost as if he had been looking for something specific. But what? Carson didn't like the niggling feeling he had in his gut. It didn't seem like a petty robbery. Something wasn't right.

Molly stretched long and let out a big yawn. She hadn't expected Carson to be there when she woke up, but still she felt a little disappointed that he wasn't. She'd never had morning sex before and if the women's magazines she'd read were correct, it could be delicious.

Giggling at her newfound sophistication in the sexual arena, Molly untangled herself from the sheets and went looking for the courtesy robe. When she stood, however, she almost sat right back down on the bed. The muscles in her thighs and her groin area were protesting at the sudden movement.

Well! She thought with a hint of pride and another giggle. Here was another new concept. He'd certainly made love to her enough in one night for her body to be sore and the idea delighted her further. She was a real woman now! And she wanted to declare it to the world!

The note was on the nightstand and she read it several times.

> *Good morning, My Molly. I*
> *hated to pull myself from*
> *your beautiful, warm body,*
> *but I have to go to work. I*
> *will find you today. I miss*
> *you already.*
> *Yours, C.*

She held it to her heart, feeling like a young schoolgirl who had just gotten her first love note. It was ridiculous, but she didn't care. She wondered where he was and what he was doing.

Glancing at the clock put her in shock – it was almost noon! She wanted to find him – if only to gauge her own feelings after their magnificent night of love.

Quickly, she moved to the shower to cleanse the sex from her body. Again she let out a squeal of delight at the very idea. Sex! Ha! Despite the little sleep and the ache in her body, she was deliriously happy.

Molly made her way to the lobby and found Carson at the Concierge desk, surrounded by security officers. Alarm registered immediately as she hastened her step toward him. When she saw that he was in one piece, she physically relaxed.

His eyes met hers and for the first time that morning, he smiled. Her face was flushed and her lips were swollen, despite the crisp new sundress she wore in an attempt to look decent. She looked like she had just spent a night making love and he felt a wave of possessive pride at the idea that he had put that content look in her eyes.

As if on cue, the guards moved away and allowed Molly to approach the desk.

"Are you ok?" she asked, a look of concern on her face.

"Yes. But someone tossed my suite."

"Tossed? You have a suite?" She was confused and she knew she badly needed a cup of coffee.

"Tossed. Turned it over. Searched it." His expression was dark again. "And yes, I have a suite here."

"Oh. I didn't know." Well, where did she think he lived? She asked herself. Frankly, she hadn't even thought about it.

"Was anything stolen?" She refused to think what might have happened had he been in the room at the time. It was unthinkable.

"A couple of things – no big deal. What bothers me is that they were obviously looking for something."

A frown of concentration creased his forehead. All morning he had been thinking of what the burglar could have wanted. He thought of the plans on his computer that were of his next hotel in Tahiti, but shook his head. That seemed too outrageous. Why would anyone want those? Besides, his laptop had been left alone.

"Do you need help cleaning it up?"

"Nah. Thanks, though. Housekeeping is probably finished by now."

Wondering how she could help him during this awful situation, Molly just sat down with a plop in the chair opposite him. "Is there anything I can do to help?"

Molly was – what was the term – wringing her hands. He'd never actually seen anyone do that before. Seeing her concern made him smooth out the worry on his face for her benefit.

"You can have lunch with me – take my mind off of it." He looked her up and down suggestively and was rewarded with her blush.

"Ok. I really need a cup of coffee anyway!"

He rose and took her arm in his. "How 'bout the garden room?"

It was a small dining room that overlooked the lavish gardens and had a small pool of fish next to the tables. At her nod, they headed in that direction. When they turned a corner and found themselves in a deserted hallway, Carson pulled her into his arms for a long, lingering kiss.

"Good morning," he said gruffly.

"Good morning," she smiled up into his gaze. Her stomach did a turn and she felt weakened from his kiss. It seemed that her body – now that it knew what delights were to be had – responded strongly to his touch. With a touch of her hand, she discovered that his did as well.

"We better get you some food." He said into her ear. "You're going to need your energy."

"Oh my!" she exclaimed, feigning a fan to her face.

Her prudish response to his suggestion made him throw back his head with laughter. To think that she could be so deliciously puritan after what they had shared, tickled his funny bone. She continued to charm him.

The kid watched as they went into the restaurant, his frustration mounting with every passing second. It wasn't about the money anymore. He needed to deliver the package or he was a dead man, it was as simple as that. And if there was one thing he valued above money, it was his own life. He knew they would be in the restaurant for at least an hour, which gave him plenty of time. He had to get that damned watch today. Shaking his head, he made his way to the elevators. The stolen master key would work just fine, he thought.

Lunch was a delicious chicken Caesar salad with fresh baked rolls and macadamia nut cheesecake. Molly ate nearly every drop on her plate and blushed when she realized that Carson was watching her with amusement.

"It was good," she shrugged, sheepishly.

"I think you were hungry."

"I think I'm still hungry – but not for food." She had never flirted and teased about sexuality and despite the heat in her cheeks, she was enjoying it.

"Let's go." He almost toppled the table when he stood up eagerly, causing Molly to laugh out loud.

When they were back in the elevator, memories of the feverish ascent the night before added fuel to the fire.

"I want you, Molly," Carson lifted her hair and kissed the nape of her neck, sending a tingle of anticipation down her spine.

As they approached her room, alarm bells went off for Carson. For the second time that day he found the door ajar and he silently motioned for Molly to stand behind him. He opened the door slightly and walked into the room, leaving Molly outside the door wringing her hands in fear.

She poked her head in when he said, "Whoever it is, I think he's gone –" he spoke too soon, however, for a short, young kid burst from the bathroom and slammed out of the room brushing roughly past Molly, pushing her out of the way. Carson took off after him, but the kid was quick. He was out the exit, down the stairs before Carson could even reach the stairs.

He grabbed a stunned Molly by the upper arms and looking searchingly over her. "Are you ok?"

She nodded and he touched her face, her hair, her body.

"Really, Carson," she said when she found her voice. "I'm ok."

He drew her into a quick, relieved hug and then reached for his cell phone, strapped to his belt. He called Harvey on his cell phone, telling him to dispatch his guards at the exits below.

"I have to go," he said hastily, kissing her on the lips.

"But-" She wanted to tell him that she thought she recognized the kid from the one who was rude to her in the shop just yesterday.

"Stay here and bolt the door. I'll come back as soon as I can." With that he swiftly left the room and headed towards the elevators.

With any luck, they had caught the culprit below.

"He slipped by, Boss," Harvey was scratching

his head when Carson approached.

One of their young guards was on the floor with a hand to his head. Leilani came forward with an icepack.

"Knocked poor Johnny here flat as he ran past."

"Did anyone get a good look at him?" Carson asked the team.

"I did," said Johnny. "He has a young face – looks about seventeen. But his eyes – he could be forty with those eyes. Brown hair, I think. Black eyes. Kind of beady."

"Good job, Johnny. We'll get the police over here for your statement and then take the rest of the day off," Carson instructed. "Is the doc in? He should look at his head. Make sure there's no concussion."

"Nope. It's his day off. He went to Honolulu."

"Then I'll ask Miss Carson to take a look at him. She's a nurse."

Carson dialed her room from the lobby and she picked up before it finished its first ring.

"Hello?"

"Hi Molly. Can you come down here and take a look at one of our guards? He has a bump on his head."

"Of course – did you get him?"

"No. But at least we have a description."

Sighing, Molly agreed to come right down.

With a borrowed flashlight to check his pupils, Molly could tell that Johnny didn't have a concussion. He did have a good lump on his head, however, and she instructed him to continue the ice and take two Tylenol as needed.

Carson watched her examine the boy with

tender concern, as she badgered him lightly about his bravery. For the second time in two days, he imagined her with children – his children and he felt as if he'd been punched in the stomach. Forcing himself to change his thinking immediately, he turned to Harvey.

"What next?" He asked. He sorely wanted to get his hands on that kid for putting Molly in danger. Though now that he was thinking a bit more clearly, he realized that he was after some*thing*, not someone. Still, the idea that she might have come back to her room without him unnerved him. He couldn't fathom the consequences.

"I recognized him," Molly said, straightening for a moment.

All three men looked at Molly with blank faces.

"I saw him in the store yesterday. He was reading an old comic book and blowing bubbles with his gum. I smiled at him but he just kind of sneered at me." She looked into space for a second before adding, "I remember thinking how strange it was that he was hanging out in such an up-scale store."

Harvey looked questioningly at Carson, who shook his head briefly indicating that she wasn't to be involved.

"We'll have Johnny go down to the police station and look through mug shots; have a drawing made based on his description of the guy. Miss Carson can corroborate it once it's complete. I'm afraid that's all we can do for now, Boss." Harvey chewed on the end of his pen, craving a cigarette.

"Good job, Harvey."

Molly finished up with a blushing Johnny, telling him to make sure he got plenty of rest and if there was a problem, to come see her right away.

She gave him her cell phone number too.

"I got away. But there was no watch. She must have it on her person," The Kid was talking to the man who had hired him to do what he had thought was a simple job. Deliver the watch to a specified location. But the stakes were raised when the chase began.

"Then get it off her person," the words were spoken low and menacing, his exact meaning understood by the kid. "I don't care what you have to do, Kid, you understand?"

Gulping, he nodded into the phone. "I'll call you when I get it," he hung up his cell phone. Damn. This job was getting worse by the minute, he thought, his nerves stretched tightly.

Carson walked Molly back to her room and they both looked around with frustration. Her room had also been tossed. Her usually drawers were now open, clothing hanging out and strewn all over the floor. Whatever he was after, it had something to do with the both of them.

"What do you think he wanted?" Molly seemed to read his mind. She seemed calm and cool as she began putting her things back in order.

"I can't figure it out. But whatever it is, it has to do with both of us."

Absently, he helped her pick up her clothing. He stood holding her cotton panties in one hand and a sundress in the other, lost in thought.

"I think you should move into my suite." The words were out of his mouth before he had a chance to think it through. He had rarely divulged that he had a suite at the hotel to a woman, let alone invite her to move in! It was ridiculous. But it was right and the moment he said it, he knew that's what he wanted.

"I don't know, Carson…" She looked at him uncertainly. Warning signals went off in her head. She feared that her heart would not be able to remain detached if they were in the same vicinity for a long period of time. She was already having trouble with her vow of no expectations.

She looked away from him.

"It makes sense. You're not safe here any more and at least there is added protection. We have an alarm on my floor and we've posted a guard."

When she didn't seem like she was going to capitulate, he went to her and took her gently by the shoulders. "I would feel better if I knew you were safe, Molly."

He looked so concerned, so protective, that she gave in. "Maybe just for a few days."

He pulled her close with relief and gratitude. Feelings he promised himself to review at a later time.

"I'll send housekeeping for your things."

"Oh, that reminds me!" Reaching in her beach bag, she pulled out the watch she had given him yesterday. "I forgot to give this back to you."

Carson eyed the package with serious thought. She picked up on his line of thinking and, with wide eyes, she asked him, "do you think he wants this watch?"

Carson nodded. "It's the only material thing linking us. He probably saw you buy it and thought you'd given it to me. That's why he went to my room first."

"It makes sense. But why? It's just a regular diving watch."

"Let's see if the police know."

Carson called Harvey again and explained their theory. The police chief was already on his way over.

"Look, Molly." Carson said as they reached the top floor on the elevator. "I think you should stay here until we figure this thing out."

Annoyed that he thought she was just a helpless female, she crossed her arms. "Why?"

He unlocked the door to his suite and motioned her to enter.

She immediately forgot what she had been saying when she entered this new, fabulous world of his. It was huge! There were four bedrooms and a large living room connected to a formal dining room and kitchen. The fixtures were all crystal and brass and there was marble on the entryway floor. The wall facing the ocean was anything but a wall. It was entirely made up of window so that you could see the view unencumbered from any direction. Sliding glass doors led out onto a large lanai, where there was oversized patio furniture and fire pit in the center. The view was magnificent!

The furniture was both opulent and comfortable at the same time. It was perfect for him.

As she looked around, she realized then that he must be horribly rich and she felt a little ashamed of herself. She didn't want him thinking she was after him for his money. She had her own money and thought maybe she should tell him. She didn't know what to do, because she'd never had a...a lover before.

He saw the transformation as she took it all in...the shock...then the wonder...then the reality. He was not one to show off his wealth, which was why he rarely had anyone in his suite. Women, he found, changed when they knew he had money. Often they became more interested in him and pushy.

Molly, he could tell, was intimidated. She had probably never seen such wealth before and she didn't know what to do with it. She was so easy to read.

"Molly," he went to her for comfort – his or hers, he wasn't sure.

She pulled away from him and turned to face him with new determination.

"I think you should explain yourself, Carson."

She acted as though his money were a dirty thing and he felt like he was a child in trouble.

"Who are you?"

"Ok. You're right. I owe you that much." Sighing, he ran a hand through his hair. "Molly, I didn't *just* design this hotel."

Her expression was puzzled, but he could see the wheels turning in her pretty head.

"My last name is Waverly. I own this hotel."

Her mouth formed an O as realization set in. He was richer than she could imagine. Of course he owned this hotel – it was obvious how everyone catered to him and hurried to do his bidding. She should have figured it out before. She thought then of the other Waverly hotels…New York, San Francisco, Chicago, Phoenix, Cape Cod…

"Why didn't you tell me? Or did you think I already knew?"

He shrugged. "It wouldn't have been that unusual. I've been written up in many magazines."

"So you thought I was interested in you for your money?" Heat rose to her face.

"I'll bet you got a good chuckle out of that one. Poor, little country nurse thinking big for a change!"

He realized then that not once had he thought that of her. She was too sincere, too real to be a gold digger. But he had met them before and they could be pretty convincing in their innocence.

"No, Molly. I didn't think that of you. But I've had to be cautious."

She tried hard understand, really, she did. "Carson, I don't care about your money. Except –"

She was working through it. Silence was the way to encourage her, so he resisted the urge to go to her as she paced in front of the window.

"Except that maybe I understand you a little better. And I am a little intimidated. That silly watch I gave you!" She was embarrassed by her meager gift. "You probably have a whole case of Rolexes!"

He moved to her and pulled her into his arms.

"Molly, that watch you gave to me meant more than any gift I've ever gotten. Don't minimize it." He gazed at her until she nodded in agreement, though she thought he was just being kind.

She didn't want him to hold her just then and she wasn't sure why. Distance was needed at that moment, so she pulled away again.

Carson prompted her. "You think you understand me better?"

"I think so. You don't trust women - that I knew right away. But maybe you fear commitment because you would never really know if she loved you for you or for your money. And maybe you think she would someday leave you – like your mother did sort of - and take half your money. Maybe I'm wrong..." she was apologizing and when she turned, she could see that she wasn't completely wrong.

He looked as if he'd been struck. She shouldn't have spoken so freely and instantly she regretted it.

"Oh, Carson, what do I know? I'm just a dowdy, old nurse from Idaho!" She tried to make light of it and she could see his struggle to move past her comments. The wall went up and his face went blank. She wished she could take back her hastily blurted analysis of him. Darn it!

"We should go downstairs now. The police are probably here."

She nodded to him and followed his lead out the door. There was an awkward tension in the air.

Despite the fact that he so easily read people and was good at dispensing his own brand of evaluation, he didn't seem to like it when it was done to him. It was unlike her to speak so openly and freely and she was wrong. She'd hurt his feelings and deeply regretted it.

10

The police chief came to investigate the crimes that had taken place that day at Carson's hotel. They presented him with the watch, their only possible clue in the case. The chief took it with him, promising to examine it thoroughly and to get back to them the next day with an update.

Carson was still guarded around Molly, so she allowed him to make an excuse that he had work to be done.

"Harvey will show you how the alarm works and will give you your own key. I'll be in my office, if you need me."

He left her without another word, more evidence that he was unhappy about her unwelcome invasion of his inner space earlier.

She followed Harvey and was amazed to find that her things had already been moved and unpacked in the guestroom of Carson's suite. The guestroom.

Disappointment washed over her at the realization that Carson must have instructed housekeeping not to move her into his own bedroom. She tried to rationalize the instant rejection she felt. But no matter how she tried, she couldn't ignore the fact that he held her at arms' length. She had told him she had no expectations, so she'd better change this self-destructive line of thinking right now!

Molly had leapt ahead to an assumption she had no business making. If she was going to make it through this wonderful affair with her heart in tact *and* be a sophisticated woman, she'd better toughen up a little.

Changing into her swimsuit, she eyed herself in the mirror. This suit was dowdy, just like the *old* Molly, she thought. It wasn't her any more. The *new* Molly was a sophisticated women who was having an affair. She giggled at the notion.

She needed to update her appearance, but wasn't sure how to do it. She had read articles about women using shopping as therapy and decided to give it a whirl. She covered her suit with a smart shorts outfit and grabbed her bag. She was going shopping!

She stopped at the main offices, hoping to enlist Leilani's help in her makeover, but was told that she was in a meeting that would last for most of the day. It didn't deter Molly, however, as she walked purposely down the path toward the shops she'd visited just yesterday.

The shop clerk was only too happy to help Molly replace her boring suit with one more colorful and a dash racier. She tried on a dozen or so before she settled on a high cut, royal blue number, which lifted her breasts to the world. It made her hold her breath with a combination of embarrassment and pride, but she hoped that Carson would appreciate it.

Next, she entered the lingerie store she had so carefully avoided during her other shopping excursion. She wanted to get rid of her ridiculous white panties and bras, but had no idea what to buy. Again a kind shop clerk helped her pick out several items that were lacy, yet still a little conservative. To her they seemed wildly provocative and she couldn't wait to feel them against her skin. As an afterthought, she grabbed a cream silk teddy and short matching robe and brought them into the dressing room. She looked…well, slutty, she figured, which was definitely something a man would appreciate.

She bought all her purchases and couldn't wait to get back to the hotel. She'd been gone for over three hours – it was a luxury of shopping in which she never indulged.

While Molly walked back along the plant-lined corridor with a little pep in her step, she inhaled the tropical scents around her. She felt great.

Then, hands reached out from a bush as she walked by and pulled her roughly into the bushes, sending her packages flying this way and that. She caught a glimpse of the boy-man as she struggled with him. He was strong.

The man got the upper hand and pushed her down to the ground onto her stomach behind a large, floral plant. He twisted her arm behind her back to hold her there as he straddled her. He was not heavy, but the pressure on her tummy made it difficult to breathe.

"Don't say a bloody word," he whispered in her ear. "I have a knife and I'd hate to have to mess up that pretty face of yours."

She nodded her acquiescence and forced herself to release the tension in her shoulders to show him she gave in. As a result, he released the pressure a bit. He grabbed the bag that was still around her shoulder and tugged it off, roughly. He dug around furiously and finally, dumped the entire contents on the ground beside her.

"Where is it?"

She knew he was talking about the watch, but she was too afraid to say anything as she gathered her wits about her. *Think, Molly, think.* She willed herself to breathe evenly. He might kill her even if she had the watch. She couldn't seem to think of anything at the moment, except for Carson's face, which flashed before her. She regretted her words to him earlier that day. She wanted to tell him she was sorry she'd made such invasive assumptions about him, but now it might be too late.

"Where's the fucking watch?" It was a whispered shout, and spit came from his mouth as he began to unravel. He pulled roughly at her hair, twisted around his hand and drummed her face into the ground to emphasize his point.

Molly's head swirled with pain and she felt blood trickling down her eyebrow. Flashbacks to that horrific night years ago in college, swept over her, leaving her shaking with fear. If only she could get the upper hand for a moment…

"I – it's with the police." She finally found the courage to speak, hoping that he would release her.

"Liar!"

He turned her over roughly and finally she could see his familiar face close up. Johnny had been right. His youthful face made him seem like a teenager, but looking closely, she could see many more years in the depths of his black eyes. His anger was palpable and she thought there was something else also – fear perhaps.

He grabbed the front of her shirt and hauled her partly up, his hand forming first a fist and then, as if he rethought it, he used the back of his hand to hit her across the face. Lips collided with teeth and she could taste the blood that pooled in the inside of her lip.

"I told you – we gave it to the police!" Her eyes begged him to let her go, but he pulled out the knife he had talked about before.

They both heard the child before either one of them made their next move. He grabbed her by the hair and pulled.

"Get up," he whispered, waving the knife to warn her. He pushed her farther into the bushes and held a hand over her mouth as the child and his mother passed by on their way back from shopping.

Molly didn't want that innocent child hurt, so she didn't even bother to try to cry out for help. But their timing was a stroke of luck for her; because now she felt like she could fight him, even a little, better than she could on the ground. The knife was the first concern, she thought.

The kid was focused on making sure the two strangers were completely out of earshot. It was a moment too late when he realized he'd loosened his grip on Molly. She elbowed him as hard as she could in the stomach and sent the attached fist down to his groin. He doubled over and grabbed at his privates, as the knife flew out of his hand. She brought her knee up as hard as she could to his chin with a slam, knocking him out completely.

Using his knife, she cut along the bottom of his ragged T-shirt and created a means by which to tie his hands. She turned him over and tied his hands behind his back.

She gathered her belongings, straightened out her clothing, tried to smooth out her hair and waited for him to awaken.

"Harvey, where's Miss Carson?" Carson was pacing his suite, his cell phone in one hand, binoculars in the other. He looked out over the grounds and couldn't see her anywhere. He'd come back to the suite to be with Molly to talk about their earlier issue, but found it empty. That was almost two hours ago and now he was beyond worry.

"I left her in the suite, sir. She said she was going to take a nap."

"Well, she's not here. I want her found – NOW!"

"Of course. I'll call you back."

Carson was not going to wait a minute longer. He raced out of his suite intent on finding Molly.

Once in the lobby, Carson saw that the guards were running off in various directions, each assigned to find Molly. He knew he should trust Harvey to handle it, but worry burned in his gut. Something was terribly wrong. He didn't like it.

Carson felt guilty for being so sensitive when Molly so accurately dissected his life. For once, he was being totally honest with himself and he didn't like what he found. She was correct. He did keep women at arms' length for a variety of reasons.

After the events of the morning, he wanted desperately to be with Molly, to talk about his self-discovery thanks to her. He felt certain that she was instrumental in helping him toward a new life. He wanted to hold her and bury himself deep insider of her again. Where the hell was she?!

A half hour passed and soon all the guards were back. There was no sign of Molly.

"A clerk at the swimming store helped Molly pick out a swimsuit," one of the guards said, still out of breath. "She hasn't seen her for over at least an hour."

Another guard added, "and the clerk at Lacy Things helped her buy – er, well, things a about an hour ago – so she must have gone there next."

Shaking his head, the guard looked at Carson apologetically, "but she was the last person that has seen her, sir."

"She couldn't have disappeared!" Carson swore long and loud, surprising his team. "Let's trace the route back to those stores and search every inch. And someone go through the security footage. Let's go!"

The men turned back toward the path to the shops, when in unison, they all stopped dead in their tracks.

There she was – packages and all – holding a knife to the kid who walked in front of her, his hands bound behind his back. Her hair was all over the place, her usually meticulous clothing smudged and rumpled, and dried blood at her forehead and lip. No one said a word for a second, but just stared at the oddly amazing sight.

Carson was frozen in the grips of conflicting fear, amazement and protective instincts.

Harvey reacted first and ordered his guards to take the criminal into their custody. They raced forward and grabbed him. The kid struggled but there was not much he could do with a foggy head and hands tied behind his back.

He glared at Molly and shouted "BITCH" as they dragged him to the security office to wait for the police.

Carson went to Molly and pulled her into his arms. She dropped her bags and the knife and let him hold her close. She caught her breath, a sob escaping at last. Now that she was safe, a wave of trembling overtook her and she had difficulty breathing.

Carson held her away from him so he could see her and assess her injuries. "Oh God, Molly!"

He lifted her into his arms and marched towards the elevators.

"Harvey…Gus – send someone with a first aid kit and call Doc," he ordered, certain without looking, that he had been heard.

The entire lobby witnessed the chivalrous swoop of Molly and the employees whispered to each other. They wondered about their boss and his uncharacteristic behavior. Soon the stories were flying.

Leilani watched with a knowing smile as Carson carried Molly off. *He has it bad,* she thought, with a smile to herself and a nod of approval.

"Put me down, Carson! I can walk." She was

appalled at his bold behavior in front of his employees. "Carson!"

But his jaw was locked in stubborn refusal to stop and let her walk. Silently, he held her all the way up the elevator while looking straight ahead. His stony silence began to worry her.

Once inside the suite, he turned – not toward the guestroom as she assumed – but toward the master bedroom, where he gingerly set her on the massive bed. The bed sank with their weight and she felt immediate comfort when she was assaulted by his scent on the down pillow.

He bent over to examine her face closely, gently turning her head to each side to see the damage. Bruises, blood and a cut on her forehead. It was grim, but could have been so much worse.

"Oh God, Molly," he leaned his forehead against her as a lump worked up and down in his throat. The terror he felt at seeing her like this and thinking the unthinkable, tore at him. He felt responsible for her safety on so many levels. Professionally, yes, but mostly as a man protecting his woman. He felt like he'd let her down and he was enraged with himself and his staff.

"I'm ok, Carson," she could feel the conflict raging in him; feel his fear and she wanted to reassure him. They were both safe now and that's all that mattered.

"Carson." She repeated as she tried to get his attention, but his eyes were closed and he seemed an immovable force. "Carson?"

He looked at her after several seconds, feeling somewhat under control. "Tell me what happened, Molly."

He assumed the worst, that she'd been raped, and her disheveled clothing supported his assumption.

She realized then what he thought and spoke quickly to explain what happened.

"He jumped out at me from the bushes and held me down on my belly so I couldn't move. He demanded the watch."

Molly's voice broke and Carson eased up off the bed to go get her a glass of water.

She accepted the water gratefully. She nodded and continued. "There was a child and his mother. They walked by and the guy dragged me up by the hair and pulled me deeper into the foliage so they wouldn't see us. He – he had a knife and told me to keep quiet."

Carson let out a frustrated growl-sigh.

"How? Molly, how did you get him?" He was unable to comprehend what she had been through – what she had done. His heart ached to just hold her and get past this, but he had to know first.

"I surprised him with a few of my moves."

"Moves?" She had moves?

"Well, after my little…incident in college, when I moved to San Francisco, Roger made me take a self defense class with him. He said "we girls" need to be able to protect ourselves. So – being a bit obsessive, I took it again on my own…six times."

She tried to grin through her swollen lip at how silly it sounded, even if it had come in handy today.

"Six times?"

"Well, I kind of liked the empowerment it gave me. Roger teased me that I should just take karate and train correctly, but I like the street self-defense. I'm quite a pro, you know."

She looked proud of herself and he felt his

worry decrease somewhat.

"Anyway, when the two people walked by, he got distracted and I took advantage of the moment. He's not very good, you know."

"But you're hurt," he touched her swollen lip with his thumb. She remembered the kid's threat to cut her face and shivered. She was grateful that she only had a few injuries.

"Yes. I'm hurt a little, but he's arrested, so I guess I win, don't I?" She tried again to smile, but her lip cracked with the attempt. "Ouch," she said with a chuckle.

A soft knock sounded at the door. "Come in," Carson called, his gaze still intent on Molly's face, taking in every detail. It was Gus.

"It's me, sir. I brought the first aid kit. Doc is on his way." Discreetly, he bent to lay it on the table out in the dining room.

"Can you bring it in here, Gus?"

Earlier, as soon as Carson and Molly had exited the lobby, employees descended on Harvey and Gus, snooping for information about the couple. Without answering their questions, Gus retrieved the first aid kit and turned toward the elevators.

Everyone stopped their badgering when someone cried "Gus?!"

He turned back to the gathering crowd and said with his usual grace, "I'll see what I can find out." With a grin, he spun on his heel.

Now, standing in the doorway of the bedroom, the only thing he could determine was that here were two people who were very much in love. Their heads were bent towards each other as they whispered intimately between them.

He'd never before seen Carson with such raw emotion on his face and his fatherly love for the boy heaved in a happy twinge. Miss Carson seemed like a sweet, classy, well-grounded woman and he hoped the best for both of them.

He cleared his throat to let them know he was there and they both tore their gazes away from each other long enough to acknowledge his presence.

"Oh Gus – I don't need Doc. I'm fine," Molly insisted.

Gus nodded and looked to his boss for approval. Carson was staring intently at Molly.

"Thank you, Gus," Carson absently motioned for him to set it on the bed. Gus did and quietly left the room.

Carefully, Carson cleaned Molly's wounds.

"This hasn't exactly been a fun vacation for you, has it?" He tried to tease lightly – to get past the stark terror he still felt deep in his belly, but she stopped his hand momentarily by putting hers on it.

"I would do it again," she admitted gravely. "Some things were not very pleasant…but some…" she was thinking of their wonderful, glorious night together. He thought of it too. "I still want you, Carson," she whispered, her lips inches from his.

"Molly," he groaned in need. He considered it, truly he did. But her lip was swelling with every passing moment and he couldn't rid himself of a new protective feeling for her that had developed. He had to think about these latest developments – had to clear his head. And he thought he'd be a scumbag to take advantage of someone in her condition, whether she desired it or not. "I can't – not while you're hurt."

"I'm not that hurt. Just my face." She

attempted to be alluring as she laid a hand on his thick thigh and leaned in. "That's not the part of my body I want you to make love to."

He wanted to take her in his arms and crush her to him, but he didn't. His face took on a new resolve as he continued to apply first aid to her injuries. His silence was answer enough.

Molly felt rejected. Maybe he was still thinking about their earlier conversation. She was silent, though her eyes pooled with unshed tears.

"Molly…" he laid her back on the bed and took her gently into his arms. "Shhh, baby. Let's just rest, ok? It's been a helluva day."

11

Darkness crept past the gauzy curtain when she stirred. She didn't want to wake Carson as he slept peacefully next to her. His strong jaw was relaxed in sleep making him seem no less powerful and the deep lines around his eyes were softer. When had she let him into her fiercely protected heart? When had she known that he would ruin her for future men, as no one would ever compare to this man? When had she fallen in love?

The idea took root in her conscious and slowly grew like the arms of a vine into a certain knowing. She closed her eyes against the onslaught of feelings. It was wrong – she shouldn't feel this way about this wonderful, free man. He wouldn't want her love, in fact may have already been thinking of a way to let her down gently. He'd warned her, hadn't he?

The memory of his rejection of her advances earlier coupled with this new realization had her head aching. She felt the need to flee before he had the opportunity to hurt her. Before she would do something foolish – as she was sure women before her had – and beg him to become hers completely.

Her head ached and her lips throbbed. And worse of all, Carson didn't want her anymore.

Gathering herself, she pulled away from him and crept from the bed. She couldn't sleep any more and she didn't want to wake him.

Carson woke up past midnight and immediately reached out to Molly. He wanted to hold her. When he found the sheets cool and empty, he pulled himself through the fog of sleep to sit up. He stumbled his way around the suite, turning on lights until he found her.

She was curled up under the light covers of the queen bed in the guestroom. He crouched down beside her and watched her sleep for a long moment.

Her lip and forehead were purple with angry bruises and he felt a stab of anger. He couldn't begin to fathom what *could* have happened to her the previous day. Gratitude that she was fine replaced the moment of anger. She was a tough little cookie, his Molly.

Her blue eyes were closed, the skin around them smooth due to a lack of exposure to the sun and maybe, because they didn't squint in laughter nearly enough. *He could change all that for her.*

The thought set him back on his bottom with surprise. He'd never thought in terms of anything more than a fun-filled affair with any of the other women he'd known. Yet here he was thinking about how he could make this one woman happy.

The part of him that clung to certain habits rejected the idea so strongly that he nearly said "no" into the silence. He shook his head at his quandary.

He didn't know why she left his bed.

He had rejected her earlier, but it was only because of her injuries. Perhaps he should have told her instead of remaining silent, but he'd held so precariously to the rock of his control, that he hadn't. Her unshed tears could have been because of the days events or it could have been because of his rejection. He didn't know, nor had he asked her.

She was sensitive unlike any woman he's known and maybe he'd hurt her feelings. Or maybe he was overthinking it and it was just because he snored. Or perhaps she just didn't want to sleep with him any more.

It was all too much to think about until the light of day when he could ponder the situation completely. Then he would set things straight with her. Sighing, he turned off the light and returned to his own room.

12

The police gave Carson and Molly a complete report the next morning in Carson's office.

"We had our lab tech take apart the watch, but all we found was a chip."

"A chip?" Molly was confused.

"An integrated circuit, also known as a chip. You find them in all electronics these days. This one didn't have anything to do with the running of the watch. We'll have to send it to a special lab in Silicon Valley to have it analyzed. It will take a couple of weeks to get the results. In the meantime, we have questioned the perp and he claims he was working alone. I don't buy it, though."

They both spoke at the same time. "Why not?"

"Because he hardly seems smart enough to carry off an elaborate scheme. My guess is he's just the courier. The guys that hired him are the ones we want. But he may not even know who they are. It's not uncommon to have a third party handle transactions for the leaders."

Feeling somewhat discouraged, Carson & Molly sat in silence after the Chief left. Staring out the window, his mind on the previous day's events, Carson wished he knew what to say to Molly. She looked so fragile sitting in the leather chair, lost in her own thoughts of criminals and diabolical schemes.

He, however, wasn't thinking about the thug she had captured. He was thinking about their own predicament – the distance between them that had suddenly appeared yesterday. Not only did he not like it, he also didn't have a clue as to how to bridge it. Every part of him wanted to turn to her and apologize – for whatever he'd done. He wanted to take her in his arms and make her promises he wasn't prepared to make.

It scared the hell out of him. His body wouldn't cooperate with his heart, however, for it stood glued to the window. Perhaps now was not the time anyway.

Molly was not thinking about the thug either, but rather was experiencing her own doubt and insecurity about their situation. He'd put her in the guest room yesterday. Then he'd rejected her romantic advance – the first one she'd ever initiated in her whole life. He had only been trying to protect her and she had read much more into his invitation to stay in his room.

She felt ashamed. They had only known each other a few days, after all. He was a smart, sophisticated, rich and devastatingly handsome bachelor. She was just a dowdy nurse from Idaho. What could he possibly want with her other than a brief affair? He was probably figuring out how to get rid of her at that very moment. She would save him the trouble, she thought. And the embarrassment.

He turned at the very moment she rose and they both spoke at once, "you know –" "I think-".

Laughing awkwardly, Carson bowed slightly to Molly. "You first," he said.

"I think I should probably get my own room back. I don't want to inconvenience you any more. Now that we know it's no longer dangerous."

She stood looking at the floor, her hands a mess of wringing fingers. The swelling around her injuries was worse today, making it difficult to talk without a lisp. She felt achingly vulnerable as she stood before him, feeling like she had her heart in her hands. Couldn't he see that?

"Molly, you don't have to do that," his voice was low, his expression unreadable.

Several long moments passed as she waited to hear the words that she knew in her heart weren't coming.

"No, I do have to," she finally ended the painful silence. She tried to gather herself together. How does one gracefully end an affair such as this without looking like a complete ass?

"Really. Thank you, Carson." She looked searchingly at him, hoping that her earnest reply was believable. "I want to thank you for everything these past few days. It's all been like a dream. You were so wonderful."

Her voice started to catch and she could feel the pressure on the back of her throat.

She was ending it, he realized. He stood looking at her for a long moment, with his jaw clenched. She seemed eager to leave, but he wasn't ready to let her go. He was still frozen in place, unable to figure out what he should say.

How had it come to this? He wondered. Was their affair already at its end? With only one amazing night together? He supposed it was. She was a tourist and he was a rambler. It was destiny. Feelings of doubt were foreign to him. He was usually the one to do the leaving.

It would be unfair of him to ask her to stay when they both knew that he had nothing more to offer than a few months of great sex.

"Ok, then," Molly summoned the courage to walk toward him and, standing on a tipped toe, she kissed his rough cheek. She hated good byes, because they were too final. After what she'd been through these past weeks, it was the last word she wanted to utter. "Take care."

As gracefully as she could, she swept quickly from the room and headed to the elevator. She didn't look behind her to see if he followed her.

Once she was in the lobby, Molly walked purposefully toward the front desk, where she approached one of the valets.

"Can you please move my things back to my old room?"

Gus overheard her and motioned her to his desk.

"Hello, Miss Carson." He said with a kind smile. "Your room is no longer available. We only have one three doors down from that room. Will that be sufficient?"

Gus could see the sadness in his guest's eyes and he wondered if she'd had a fight with Carson. He couldn't imagine such a thing after what he'd witnessed the previous evening, but something had happened and it made him sad to see her trying so bravely to be strong. Carson was known to break a few hearts.

"Yes, that's fine. Thank you, Gus," she turned away and stopped at his next words.

"You don't have to move, you know. I'm sure everything will be fine." There was kindness in his voice and her back stiffened at the imminent tears.

"Yes, I do," she said just loud enough for him to hear her.

Leilani overheard her father talking to Molly and as soon as she left, Leilani descended upon her father. "What happened?" She demanded.

"I don't know."

"Molly's moving out of Carson's room? But she just moved in!" She stood with her hand on her slender hip, looking indignant.

"Stay out of it, Leila."

"But-"

"Stay out of it."

Leilani paced back and forth behind her father's desk. He was right about her minding her own business, but she considered Molly her friend as well as Carson. It couldn't hurt to at least let Molly know she was available to talk with if she needed her. Deciding on a game plan, she left her father, who simply sighed and watched her go.

Back in Carson's suite, Molly finished her packing. She wandered around the large suite touching this and that. She liked the décor – it was so like Carson. Masculine, yet classical and carefree. The whole suite smelled faintly of his musky cologne and when she came to his bedroom, she couldn't resist plunging her face into its cool softness and taking a long inhale.

In his rooms, she could feel his powerful presence and even with his absence the place didn't seem so empty. She would miss him more than she was able to admit at that moment.

The soft knock on the door brought her out of her reverie with a long sigh. Carson stood behind the valet and for a moment, Molly brightened.

For a half a second, Molly felt hope. Perhaps he *did* want her. Perhaps he was going to ask her to stay. But unfortunately, he only stood watching silently.

The valet moved efficiently when she pointed to her bags, but she didn't take her eyes off of Carson. She tried a small smile, but his response was cool and distant.

He barely moved aside as she followed the valet out of the room, their bodies grazing gently as she passed, muttering a breathless, "excuse me."

Before the door closed, she turned back to him and searched his eyes. Nothing.

Politely, she said, "thank you, Carson." And then she was gone.

Carson used to like being alone in his own place. It was his refuge, his territory. But today, the faint smell of Molly drove him from the suite, back to work.

He felt an overwhelming urge to make his arrangements to get away again. He had some time before his next project was going to start and his hotels were running smoothly, so he put his mind on the task of deciding what he was going to do next.

Maybe he needed his own vacation. A chance to do something new...go someplace he hadn't been before. God knows he needed a place where he could escape from this ache in his heart...someplace where he wasn't likely to meet up with a nurse from Idaho.

"You're leaving, aren't you?" Leilani found Molly at the pool, soaking up more of the penetrating Hawaiian sun.

Molly removed her sunglasses and drew her eyes up – all the way up – to meet the eyes of her new friend. She looked back down at her book and put the sunglasses back on. "Yes."

Leilani plopped down on the chaise next to Molly and leaned over. "What happened?!"

Molly smiled when she once again met her friend's gaze. It was the first time that Leilani seemed like the young lady that she was. She reminded her of a petulant teen who wanted to know why a boy didn't like her.

"It's just time, Leilani."

"But I thought you were with Carson..."

"I was. It was great, but it's over. Time to move on." She sounded much braver than she felt. In fact, her heart felt empty and desolate.

"Molly, that's bullshit. I expect that kind of attitude from a man, but not from you. You're different. I like you."

Molly laid a hand on Leilani's tan forearm. "I like you too. Maybe we can keep in touch. You know, email."

Leilani grasped Molly's hand, trapping it there. "I'd like that, Mol. But what about Carson? I just don't understand."

Molly sat up, releasing her hand from her friend's grasp. She brought her knees around the lounge chair and sat facing her.

"Leila, you know Carson better than I do. He's a wonderful man to be with…charming and smart. He knows how to romance a woman and to make love…a great guy to have fun with. But he doesn't believe in love. And he doesn't want to be a keeper. I need a keeper."

"He *is* a keeper. He just hadn't found the right woman. Until you."

"You flatter me," Molly let out an empty laugh. "But what could he possibly see in a dowdy nurse from Idaho?"

"You're not dowdy, Molly Carson! And he does see something in you – the same things that I see…you're warm and bright and sweet. You're beautiful in a classic way. You have a great sense of humor and you'd do anything for a friend. Any man would be luck to have you! *You're* a keeper!"

Molly appreciated her friend's vehement attempt to convince her of her fine qualities, but even if she did believe her, she knew that she wasn't enough for Carson.

"Thank you, honey. I'm trying to believe what you say, but the truth is, I'm not sophisticated or glamorous enough for Carson. He's already bored with me. We'll both just let it fizzle out as affairs do."

God, she sounded so worldly. The end of the affair. Que sirah sirah. But in truth, it felt as if her soul were shattering apart, piece by piece.

"But-" Leilani didn't know which words to use to explain what she felt in her heart. She *knew* that they were meant to be.

"It's ok. It was good for me, actually." She swallowed back the tears that threatened. "I needed to…to…well, get laid, I suppose."

"It wasn't like that with Carson, Molly. I know him."

"Then you know that what I'm saying is true. He doesn't want to be tied down."

"You love him." It was said softly and with such kindness, that a single tear made it past Molly's careful guard and slid down her face.

"I don't want to love someone who doesn't want to be loved."

"But he needs you – we can all see that! And he does want to be loved – desperately, I think."

"Then I hope he finds what he's looking for."

"Stay." It was a quiet plea.

"I can't. I just can't risk my heart anymore, Leilani. I've lost too much these last weeks."

"I understand." But she didn't. She still had one more angle left to try and she was going straight to Carson's office next.

"Now tell me about that handsome man I've seen you hanging out with lately…"

Carson slammed down the phone, cursing aloud to the empty office. It was true that everything was running smoothly with his business. His family was healthy and he was a handsome, virile bachelor. He had the life every man wished for. So why did he want desperately to pick a fight with someone?

"Rough day?" Leilani leaned against the open door jam, watching his mood become darker by the moment. Very good, she thought.

"Just business."

He didn't invite her in, but she waltzed in anyway, and made herself at home across the desk from him.

"Are you sure about that?"

He didn't like her tone or the fact that she acted like she owned the damn place. "Mind your own business, Leila." It was a low growl.

Anyone else would have been frightened out of the room, but she just sat back and twirled a long clump of hair between her fingers, thoughtfully. "Hmmm."

"Hmmm what?"

"I wonder what's got you all pissy today."

"Go away. I'm busy."

"Could it be one Molly Carson?"

"Leave me alone."

"I think I hit a sore spot."

Carson threw down the pen he was clenching and rubbed two rough hands over his face. He felt like hell. The events of the previous day had taken a toll on him and it showed. But he didn't want to talk with Leilani about it, so he turned his chair to face the window, hoping she'd get the hint. He wasn't so lucky.

"She's leaving."

"So?"

"So, you shouldn't let her go."

"It's not up to me. She's a free woman."

"Carson…"

"What?!" He whirled around to face her, his face red with anger. "Why can't you just leave it alone?"

They both stood, her height matching his as she came around the desk to where he stood.

"Because I care about you, Carson. I've watched women come and go in your life and I haven't said anything…mostly because I didn't want you to be with any of them."

His jaw remained clenched for several moments before he relaxed somewhat. She was being sincere and he cared about her. "Leilani-"

"Let me finish," she turned to look out the window, aware that he was still watching her profile.

"I've always had a girlhood crush on you, Carson. I probably always will. But I know it will never happen between us. You think of me like a little sister. And Molly – well, Molly's different. She's good for you. And you're good for her."

"I'm not good for anyone," his tone was quiet and more vulnerable than she'd ever heard. "I'm a commitment phobic bastard wrapped in the body of a charming bachelor."

"That's bull and you know it. You can be anyone you want to be – I've seen you handle greater challenges than that. I just think it's a habit for you to dodge commitment. That, and the fact that you hadn't met the right woman. Until Molly."

"I don't want to be tied down. Even to someone that I like."

"Love."

"What?"

"You love her."

"No. I-" He looked so stricken at the idea that Leilani wanted to pull him into her arms and comfort him like a small boy. "I don't – I-"

"I know. I know. You don't believe in love." She rolled her eyes. "Whatever!"

"I don't. At least not the kind you're talking about and certainly not for me."

"Look, Carson, I don't know what happened to you, but I do know one thing. If anyone deserves to fall in love and live happily ever after – it's you. It's yours. You just have to reach out and take it."

She laid a hand gently on his bicep. "She loves you too, you know."

"She'll get over it." He wanted to believe her, really he did. But Molly left him. She moved out of his suite and hasn't spoken to him again. It was over.

"Will you?"

"I'm already over it. We slept together – that's it." He sounded defensive even though he was trying to sound tough. "There are plenty of women to replace her."

Leilani ignored his brash statement because she knew he didn't really mean it.

"She's leaving tomorrow. And if you're too stubborn to go to her tonight, I have her address in San Francisco."

"I don't need it."

"Good. Then you'll go to her tonight." She smiled as if it were already decided.

"No." He leaned his head against the glass. "I'm going to let her go, Leila. She deserves better than me."

"Probably. But she doesn't want anyone else."

"I'm going to let her go."

"Fine." Leilani leaned over and kissed him affectionately on the cheek. She said lightly, "Let me know when you want her address."

13

Molly found herself watching the sunset alone on the beach that evening. She couldn't remain in her room, pacing with worry and uncertainty, for one more minute. Here, on the beach where the water was calm and the sun was just dipping down over the water causing a vivid contrast of pinks and grays and purples, she knew her decision to leave was the right one.

It was time to go home and start a new chapter in her life. She couldn't stay in Kaui forever no matter how much she had come to love the beautiful, peaceful island.

Throughout the day, Molly had been on edge and it wasn't until she sat quietly on the beach that she realized she had been waiting for something. For Carson. A part of her desperately wanted him to come to her. To tell her that he didn't want her to go. To make love to her, even if it was one last time. But she was indulging in fantasy with that kind of thinking.

It was exactly as he said it would be and as she knew in her heart. It was over.

And yet, if he came to her on this last evening, knocking softly on her door, she would open to him. Her body. Her heart. She would show him what she could still not put into words. She would leave him with a tantalizing, loving image of her before leaving him for good.

Delicious desire tangled in her belly at the idea of another night spent in his arms. She knew she could go to him, but would he turn her away? She was not willing to risk it, for she was far too deep already.

She had never been in love before, and Leilani's sweet suggestion of her true feelings led her to realize that this was indeed love. She hadn't expected strong need to accompany the pure joy that she felt when she was with Carson. She'd always thought it took years to fall in love. It was naïve. She was naïve.

It was foolish that she had allowed herself to taste the one delicacy that was tantalizingly out of her reach. His absence was like a knife in her heart that tore tiny holes of emptiness.

A tear escaped her closed eyes as she felt the receding sun on her face. She couldn't blame him, she admitted. He was who he was. Just as she was who she was.

Hadn't she longed for adventure? Hadn't she wanted her predictable, boring life to change? Boy did she get what she asked for! In less than a week she'd let go of Roger, had her first affair, moved in with a man, got mugged, fell in love and got a broken heart. Good gracious, were vacations always like this? She wondered.

She'd changed this week. With that change, came the pain of letting go. But dear God, she'd do it all over again if she could.

It was time to go home, she knew, as she stood and brushed herself off. The sun had set and so had her little love affair. Dusk was on its way to darkness, which resembled the feelings in her heart.

With one last deep breath of ocean air, Molly turned back toward the hotel. She had only walked a few feet before she saw him standing there. He was a hundred or so yards away, his wavy hair moving with the breeze.

She couldn't see his face in the darkness, but she could feel the tension in his body, which was tall and rigid.

A bubble of hope percolated in Molly's center and flowed through her as she walked slowly, deliberately toward him. She didn't want to say or do anything that would take away this precious opportunity. He'd come to her and she was going to show him one last time, how his touch stirred her and brought her to life.

As she moved closer and was finally able to see his face, she saw smoldering passion in his eyes and something...something she couldn't name. She stopped before him uncertain of what to do next. Her mouth was dry with anticipation and desire, her body weak.

Carson didn't move until she was before him and even then, he waited several heartbeats before he could move. She looked beautiful with her hair slightly tangled around her face, her blue eyes dark with knowing.

Her lips were not swollen any more. That was good, because he intended to kiss those lips.

Neither one of them spoke as Carson covered the final two steps in one and pulled her into his arms, his embrace strong and a little bit rough.

She let him possess her, his lips almost savage with hunger and ignorant of her fading injuries. Her body responded to his attack with her own urgency, as she gripped his back with fierce desperation, her legs trying to climb up his strong body. Her hair was fisted in his large hand as he pulled her head back to gain better access to her lips.

Without breaking contact with her lips, he pulled her toward a secluded sandy cove hidden by green foliage, where they crashed to the sand and tore at each other's clothing. Feverish with need, Molly whimpered tiny cries of desire. She yanked his shirt over his head and reached for his pants, oblivious to the sand gathering in her long hair and into her clothing.

The light sundress was thrown up to her waist as Carson positioned himself between her open legs, ripping at the small patch of lace.

Insanity surged through him and briefly, he thought he might actually hurt her with his demanding need. The ache to be inside her was an obsession, a hunger, and his need was stronger than he'd believed possible.

Her whispered, "please, Carson" released him from doubt. She was wet and ready for him as he plunged into her despite his intention to slow down.

He took her quickly to a climax and stifled her cry with his powerful mouth. Her body arched up to him, inviting him even deeper, and he could no longer hold himself back. He poured himself into her body, his release unlike any he'd ever had before.

She cried out again as another orgasm tore through her, the sound muffled by the crashing surf.

Panting, he collapsed on top of her, thankful that her body was cushioned by the sand. He held her hair in his hand, caressing her face, her hair, her neck with gentle desperation. He needed to know she was there and that he hadn't just dreamt it. He was shaking – not from the release that making love to her had caused, but from something within himself that kept the words he wanted to say to her at bay.

Molly let him hold her and caress her as she slowly came back to reality. What she'd just experienced went beyond all imagination and her body still tingled as proof. She had let go of herself in a way that truly overwhelmed her.

When he was deep inside of her, driving and possessing her, she had given him yet another piece of herself. Her soul. She felt it as surely as she now felt his body still on top of her. She knew it couldn't possibly mean the same to him, but it was ok. She was saying good-bye to him in her own way. Tomorrow she would think and feel and probably regret. Tonight was for creating a memory that she would carry with her forever. A little gift to herself.

After several moments, Carson rolled off of her and slipped out of her warmth.

"Molly-" he didn't know what to say. He felt like an animal, like a horny teenager with only one goal in mind. It wasn't his style or his intention to take her so aggressively. Her lip had started to bleed a little bit, which compounded his guilt.

Despite all that, he would do it again, given the chance. "Molly – I'm sorry."

Finding her haggard voice, Molly tried to play it lightly. "For what? The two orgasms I just had?"

He let out a blast of air that was meant to be a laugh. "For being so...so..."

"Eager?"

He smiled. "I guess."

"It's ok. I was eager too."

He helped her to stand and straighten her dress and brush the sand off of her back and her hair. She was a sandy mess. Bending, he picked up the pair of panties that had been thrown to the side.

"Not your usual white cotton?" he twirled the scant lacy panties on one finger. Blushing, she reached for them, but he drew them away. Inhaling, he appreciated her scent and then tucked them into his pocket. "I think I'll just hold onto these for now."

Horrified and flattered at the same time, Molly raised her head defiantly, brushed briskly at her rumpled dress and marched past him to the path.

He threw his head back and laughed at her indignance. When he caught up with her, he said in a sexy growl, "how does it feel to walk around in that dress without your panties?"

Her whole body responded to his naughty reminder and her legs went weak.

Stopping to lean into him, she countered his question by teasing with a question of her own. "How is it knowing that there is nothing underneath this dress but me?"

She continued down the path.

His jaw dropped open in surprise. Again, he laughed out loud before catching up to her. He pulled her in and tucked her under his arm as they walked back to the lobby, waving to smug Gus and Leilani as they passed by.

"Stay with me tonight," he nibbled on her ear as they waited for the elevator.

She didn't have to think twice. "Ok."

Molly would stay one more night with him. She wanted it more than she had wanted anything ever. It was her last chance to be with him, she knew, and she shamefully didn't care what it said about her character.

She met his eyes. She promised herself not to think about the consequences. Not to think about tomorrow.

Because tomorrow, she was still going home.

The shower was luxurious and another new adventure for Molly. With two tall shower heads and little shower sprays all the way up and down two sides of the wall, every inch of their bodies was washed and massaged.

Carson gently shampooed Molly's hair with a look of serious concentration.

She smiled up at him, causing him to pause and search her eyes. He smiled back at her and leaned in to gently kiss her tender lips.

They ordered dinner in and while lounging in his thick bathrobes, talked throughout the meal. She openly talked about Roger and found that some of the sadness had dissipated.

Carson talked about what few memories he had of his mother, his eyes softening as he spoke. He didn't seem to harbor any resentment toward her from what Molly could see, especially since the time before and after her death had been exceptionally bad for him.

"Did your father ever remarry?"

"Yes."

"And?"

"And what?" His eyes darkened menacingly.

"And did you love her? Did she treat you well?"

"No and no."

Carson continued to eat, but Molly stopped to look a little more closely at him. "I'm sorry."

"For what?"

"That she hurt you."

"It was twenty years ago, Molly. I got over it."

She looked thoughtful. "Hmm. Getting over it and healing are two different things. I think we can *think* we put something behind us, but it's still there until we are forced to deal with it."

When Carson didn't respond, she continued.

"Take me for example. I didn't even realize that I was afraid of men until you came along."

Finally, Carson met her eyes and put down his fork. Glad to have his full attention, Molly plunged ahead. "And since you've been so good to me, I'm not afraid any more. You helped me heal even though I didn't know I needed to heal."

She touched his hand to emphasize the point.

"Thank you, Carson."

Carson wanted to tell her that she shouldn't be thanking him that she should be running for her life. But he nodded in response. On an intellectual level, he understood the point she was trying to make. Emotionally, he was not ready to go there. He was with her tonight and that was enough for now.

"I didn't do anything."

"Yes, you did. You made me see myself in another way altogether. You made me believe in the sexual woman inside of me. I didn't know that woman existed until you."

"She was there, Molly. She just needed to be encouraged a little bit." He smiled at the memory of their lovemaking on the sand only hours ago. His eyes turned smoky as he looked down into her cleavage. Blushing, she grinned back at him.

"I'll be right back," she said and grabbed her purse as she headed to the bathroom.

Previously on the way to Carson's room, Molly had stopped at her room and picked up the small bag from the lingerie store and stuffed it into her beach bag with a few other items.

She used his brush to comb out her hair and then donned the silky ensemble and examined herself in the mirror. She didn't look at all like the dowdy nurse from Idaho image that she had in her mind. It was just as he said. She felt like a woman – the woman that had been buried inside of her for years. He had encouraged her to be free.

Stepping out into the dimly lit living room, she found Carson standing at the window looking out into the night, his wine glass gently swirling in his strong hand.

He turned when he heard her enter and his breath caught. He almost dropped his wine glass.

She was exquisite standing next to the couch, her long hair swept over one shoulder as she stood confidently, seductively looking him in the eye. He gulped in air as he tried to maintain his balance.

She wore a skimpy, silky robe that outlined her ample breasts and smooth curves. He longed to know what was under the robe, if anything.

Gone was the look of uncertainty. She was all woman and she knew what she wanted.

For a moment, he felt a rush of fear and anticipation race through him. He did not want to disappoint her, now that the stakes were higher for him.

She walked slowly to him and took the glass from his hand and gently set it on the table. With an outstretched arm, she took him by the hand and brought him to the couch, where she paused long enough to unzip his shorts and let them fall to the ground.

He was all man underneath and he was already ready for her. He yanked his shirt over his head, anxious for whatever his little seductress had in mind.

Molly bade him to sit by pushing his broad shoulders with her small hands. He sat.

Purposefully, she knelt in front of him and kissed the insides of his thighs, one by one, stopping just before she reached his erection, causing him to gasp. With her eyes on his, she bent again and took him in her mouth. He held her hair out of her face so that he could witness this glorious movement of her mouth on him.

Mindful of her tender lips, she artfully tasted him with curious interest. Her lack of experience was not reflected as a lack of skill. She went on instinct, tasting him and taunting him. She brought him to the brink more than once, and then backed off by removing her mouth and kissing the insides of his legs again.

He wanted to lose himself in her mouth, but just as he was there, she drew away, leaving him tortured with arousal. When he could stand it no more, he gently pulled on her hair and reached for her free hand to bring her up to him. She let him guide her to a certain point, but then, she released his hand and stood before him.

He drank in her beauty with greedy eyes. He noticed that her once pale skin now had a glowing tan. Her hair was a twisted mess, her lips swollen from her recent project. Standing there in her woman power, she was gloriously erotic and he wanted her now.

"Molly, you're beautiful," he growled at her, but still she wouldn't let him touch her.

Standing a foot away, she slowly untied the ties to her robe and let it fall to the floor. She stood before him in the tiniest of teddies and he felt the almost nonexistent grasp of control slip from him.

He grabbed for her waist, but she giggled and broke from his embrace.

"No," she breathed. "Let me."

She took one of his large hands in hers and guided it to her breast where she only let him get a brief touch before she continued his journey down to her bottom and then around to her moist center. Easily the snaps came undone and his eyes rolled back in his head as he delved into her wetness with two strong, rough fingers.

Molly's head fell backwards at the heat he instantly drew from her with a touch of his fingers. It only took a moment before she felt herself losing control and this time she needed to be in control. She drew his hand away.

With both hands, she captured his wrists and held them on the sides of his head. Clearly, it was to be hands off for him. Concentrating, she straddled his lap and took him all the way into her.

"God, Molly." He gritted his teeth at the tortuous pace she set as she eased him in and out in a slow rhythm. His chest hair brushed against the lace of her lingerie even while her tummy slid seductively over his.

"Damn it, Molly, I have to touch you," he growled between his teeth.

She released him and he grabbed at her, his large hands covering her back, her shoulders, and her bottom. Their mouths met in a heated exchange and soon he was lifting her up and down on him. His nose nuzzled the breasts that were in his face and he tried to release one from the confines of the lacy cup. With a moan of success, he took her into his mouth and riddled the nipple with caresses from his tongue.

Molly's head moved back and forth as she increased the pace. She could feel him coming close and she wanted him there first this time. He didn't let her down. He called out her name as he came inside her with fierce release.

Breathing hard, she stopped moving and let him rest for a moment. He didn't want to rest.

Carson reached between her legs and captured the swollen nub between his thumb and forefinger, which immediately made Molly explode in her own climax.

"No fair," she whined when she came back to earth. "That was supposed to b your turn."

He grinned at her disappointment. "That *was* my turn."

He stood with her still wrapped around him and walked them to the bedroom, where he carefully deposited her on the bed. Curling her body into his, he breathed in her soft scent and slipped into a deep, satisfied sleep.

They slept, bodies tangled together until Molly woke in the early hours of morning. With a deep sigh, she looked at the clock on the table next to her. She still had a few hours before she had to leave, but as she watched Carson sleep, she knew if she didn't leave now, she might never. Staying meant drawing out the inevitable. It meant putting herself in his hands until he decided it was over. It meant opening her heart wider to her love for Carson, a risk she could not take in her current vulnerable state.

It was time to go.

She didn't want to wake him, so she quietly got herself dressed and sat at his study desk, where she wrote him a brief note.

Dear Carson,

I don't know how I'll ever thank you for all that you've done for me. Our moment in time will mean the world to me forever. But I think we both know that it's time for me to go. You will always have a very special part of me...my heart. I hope someday that you believe in love for yourself. I wish you happiness always.
Molly.

Hours later, Carson stared out the window, the note from Molly still crumpled in his hand. He'd read it over and over again, as the realization crept in. She was gone.

He'd awoken after ten, his body alive and ready to possess Molly again. Before consciousness found it's way past sleepy fog, he felt joy deep in his heart, the kind of joy that made anything seem possible. Perhaps he was beginning to believe in love. Perhaps he was as close to it as he could get. Either way, he wanted and needed Molly like he'd never needed a woman before.

Yet when he reached for her, for the second time in a week he found the bed empty, the only thing lingering to remind him she'd been there was the faint scent of her perfume.

Agonizing pain replaced the moment of joy as he searched the suite for her. But all he found was the brief note. In a rage he crumpled the note and then, hoping for a clue as to when she had left, he flattened it out and read it again. And again.

The front desk confirmed his suspicion. She had checked out and taken the first flight out of Kauai at 8:30 that morning. She was gone.

Still in a rage, he began throwing things into his travel bag as he prepared to go after her in his private jet. He tried ignoring the niggling thought in the back of his mind. She didn't want him or she would have stayed.

Anger gave way to hurt as he tossed the bag to the corner and plopped helplessly on the bed. He hadn't told her how he thought he felt about her. He thought he had time to sort through it before he made any rash decisions. It was all new territory and he needed to gain control of himself.

At the beginning when they first met and even up until last night, Carson thought he held all the cards. It never occurred to him that she didn't want anything more than an affair with him. To leave him while he was sleeping was a chicken shit way to end their affair. He felt betrayed. Used. By a conservative little nurse from Idaho, no less.

Molly cried all the way home to San Francisco. The first class flight attendant quietly brought her a box of Kleenex and a sympathetic smile. It was the right thing to do, she kept telling herself. She had to protect her heart and move on. She just wondered how long it would be before this bone deep ache faded away.

14

One Month Later

Molly stood looking around the penthouse apartment in the building that would now be hers. It had been a pleasant surprise when she found out that Roger owned the old building. Workers were hammering on the old wood floor to finally fix the creaks that had driven Roger crazy, while Molly finished painting the trim in what would be her new bedroom.

In her eyes, the four-story, stucco building with the large bay windows, was a true icon of San Francisco style and she loved it there. The feelings of loneliness due to Roger's death were fading. Certainly now she could afford to live anywhere she chose, but she liked the eclectic little community in the building and she felt at home here.

Since her return from Kauai, she had painstakingly gone through each of Roger's items and either packed them up for donation to the local charity or to send them on to his family. They could do with them as they wished.

There were a few precious items that she selfishly kept – his photo albums, his music collection and his guitar...maybe someday she would learn to play. For now it gave her comfort sitting in its old place propped up against the living room wall next to the fireplace.

Today the movers were expected to take away the old items and move her things into this space. In one corner, she had two suitcases packed for her little adventure. She was going to Italy, a dream she'd had since she was a little girl and she finally had the courage to go. It was a shame that she was going alone, but somewhere in the past few weeks, she resolved to start anew...a new life, with a new sense of adventure. She touched her belly. At least for a few months, anyway.

Nursing no longer appealed to her and she figured she was going through some sort of mid-life crisis. Funny how in some areas of life she was ahead of her time and in others, she was distinctly slow.

The room was brighter now, covered in a soft pink with off-white trim. She had chosen to paint the whole apartment herself, as a form of therapy. She enjoyed working with her hands and the physical exhaustion at the end of the day, kept her from pining over Carson.

Carson.

She had banned him from her thoughts, though at weak moments, he crept in. Like today. His energy seemed to be with her as she put the finishing touches on the huge bay window. Several times she caught herself gazing out at the water of the Bay in the distance, thinking of him and wishing he were with her...

She wondered what he would think of this old place…she figured he'd appreciate the character and the architecture, though he probably preferred the more modern structure himself. Like his hotels. It was as if he were there with her, he was so prevalent in her thoughts.

Carson stood in the doorway watching Molly paint slow, methodical strokes along the window. She didn't know he was there because loud, classical music filled the room. A couple of times, she paused and gazed out the window and wiped a rolled up sleeve along her brow. Her hair was pulled back in a ponytail and her skin had faded back to its original creamy white.

She didn't look as sad as she did right after Roger's death, but still there was a peaceful melancholy about her. She wore Capri jeans and white keds tennis shoes and he thought that she had lost a few more precious pounds since he'd seen her last. Still, she fed his hungry eyes and he couldn't stop staring at her.

Feeling guilty for watching her so long, he finally knocked gently on the side of the door.

"Yes, come in." Molly thought it was one of the workers, so she finished the line she was painting without looking in the direction of the door. "I was thinking we should focus on the faucet in the master bedroom."

She expected the worker to come forward and answer her, but when no one did, she glanced over and stood abruptly, dropping the paintbrush on the wood floor. "Carson!"

He rushed forward and took the paint towel from her hand and wiped at the floor, quickly saving the finish from a spot of white.

"Don't – you'll get yourself dirty," she found herself saying.

He looked magnificent in a dark, tailored suit and rich, silky tie. Still, he bent to clean up her mess and handed her the brush. She took it with a shaking hand and put it safely on the paint tray. She didn't wait for the towel, but wiped her hands on the oversized oxford shirt that used to be Roger's.

When the commotion was over, they stood, face to face, drinking in each other's eyes.

"Hi," he said softly to her, gently curling a stray strand of hair off of her face and over her ear, his smile warm

"Hi," Molly whispered back. Warning bells traded places with the joy of seeing him again and she stepped back. His hand dropped to his side and he became serious.

"What are you doing here?" She didn't mean to sound blunt and accusatory, but the words were out of her mouth before she could sensor them.

He looked outside the window and paused before commenting, "beautiful view."

When she didn't answer and merely stood staring at him, he met her gaze again.

"I came to see how you are. I was in town and decided look you up."

The idea that he would be in town at some point hadn't occurred to Molly. Now it seemed ridiculous that she hadn't considered it. Of course he would come to the city – he owned one of the largest, most elite hotels in San Francisco just 15 blocks from her apartment.

Molly straightened her back and summoned a weak smile. Her voice was polite as she answered him.

"I'm fine – thank you for asking. But there really was no need to come."

"Yes, there was." Carson stuck a hand in his suit jacket and produced a pair of small, gold earrings in the shape of an open rose. "I wanted to return these to you."

They were just cheap costume jewelry that Molly had bought at Target before her trip.

She realized that his sense of honor compelled him to return the earrings and not just throw them in the garbage, though he could have easily had someone on his staff mail them to her. Quickly, as if she was afraid to get burned, she scooped them out of his hand and thrust them into her own jean pocket.

"That was unnecessary, but thank you."

"You're welcome." The tension in the air was palpable and Carson filled the silence again.

He nodded in the direction of the suitcases in the corner, "you going somewhere?"

Confused, Molly turned toward the suitcases and realized what he was saying. "Oh – yes. I'm going to Italy – Florence - in a couple of days. I've rented a cute little villa for a month. I'll use it as my base and take day trips to other cities."

"Oh, I see." Confusion creased his brow. "And this is your apartment?"

"Yes, it used to be Roger's."

"Molly, how can you afford all this on a nurse's salary?"

Molly stiffened in defense.

"I have some money – Roger left me some of his estate. This building is part of that."

"I'm sorry – it's none of my business. I know how much you loved Roger. I'm sorry for prying."

This wasn't going at all how he'd imagined it and he was angry with himself for handling the reunion like a clumsy jerk.

"It's ok." She turned to reach for the brush again and with a dismissive wave, she sighed, "Well, I have a lot of work to do today. Thank you for bringing my earrings by."

Carson stood feeling like an idiot. How this woman affected him so, he couldn't understand.

"Molly – would you like to have dinner while I'm in town – before your trip?"

She stared down at her paint-stained hands, thinking for a long moment. Oh how she wanted to! But she knew the danger involved in spending any more time with him.

"I don't think that's a good idea, Carson," she said at last.

"Why?" He felt his temper stirring – how much more could this woman reject him?

"Because – I – you – we…we're not a good combination."

"Why?" He resisted the urge to grab her by the arms and shake her.

"You know why, Carson. Why are you torturing me? We want different things. It would end someday and I think we both know which one of us would end up getting hurt. I just can't go through that. I'm not like those other women you see."

She felt she had said her piece with a minimal amount of bitterness and that, relieved, he would simply walk away. She had just given him another opportunity and she fully hoped he'd take it.

"Who says it will end?" He didn't like what he was hearing and clearly she had moved on.

Molly was becoming frustrated that he wasn't making this easy for her. Didn't he see how hard this was?

Her voice rose as she crossed her arms defiantly, unaware of the paintbrush wetting her shirtsleeve. "Be real, Carson! You told me yourself that you like being a bachelor...you don't want to get tied down...you like sleeping alone. That you don't believe in love." She threw his own words back in his face. "You were crystal clear about what you want in life - I got it, ok? Now I'm giving you the opportunity AGAIN to just walk away. I wish you would take it and just leave me alone!"

He took a step forward and she held the paintbrush out like a shield. He didn't give a damn. He grasped her upper arms and pulled her into him and kissed her ruthlessly, in an attempt to melt every defense she had constructed.

Angrily, she pushed him away, smearing his coat with paint. Neither noticed.

"What have you done to me, Molly Carson?" He growled as he wiped at his mouth.

"Excuse me," one of the movers stood apologetically at the door. "I don't mean to interrupt," he said sheepishly. "But where do you want this stuff?"

Molly turned to him, "that's ok, we're finished. I'll show you the guest bedroom."

With barely a backward glance, she tossed over her shoulder, "good-bye, Carson".

She disappeared down the hall and Carson took a moment to get himself together before he turned and left the apartment. He should feel relieved, he thought. She was right. He didn't want any attachments. He liked being single. And she deserved to have what she wanted – a home, a family and a man who didn't want to run at the first sign of commitment. He wished to God he was that man, because she was the closest thing to perfect for him than he'd ever encountered. He was honest with himself and he knew that it was a stretch. A stretch he'd have to think long and hard about reaching.

Molly waited in the other room until he was gone. The calm closure one expected to feel at a final good-bye never came. In its place, a desperate sadness engulfed her heart as she sank to the floor.

Would she ever be able to fill the emptiness that his absence created in her? Was she wrong to keep the secret of the new life blossoming inside of her from Carson? She would have plenty of time to think about it while she was gone.

15

Traveling to Europe proved to be more exhausting than Molly had anticipated, even if she was doing it all first class. The long flight left her legs and feet so swollen that she could barely fit into the sandals she had slipped off during the flight. She discovered once again that she was unable to sleep on an airplane, and her stomach was doing somersaults, so she arrived in Florence more jet lagged and cranky than she expected. Luckily, her personal driver greeted her and drove her to the villa just outside of the main city.

It was a beautiful, quaint little one-bedroom cottage with a flower garden and white stucco fence for privacy. Like most buildings in Europe, it was centuries old but well maintained. There were a basket of fresh breads and a bottle of Chianti waiting for her in the kitchenette.

The bedroom had a large, four-poster bed made up with an old-fashioned yellow, flower quilt and soft, down pillows. Gauzy drapes parachuted the windows in the light Italian breeze. It was perfect. She didn't bother to unpack or change clothes, but simply laid on the bed and fell fast asleep.

Molly awoke the next morning feeling completely refreshed and ready to explore. Having pre-arranged for the driver to pick her up at noon, Molly had enough time to unpack, shower and eat a smal breakfast before he came. With a deep breath, she stepped from the cottage to begin her adventure in Italy.

Carson couldn't concentrate on his work, even a week after he'd seen Molly looking vulnerable and adorable in her San Francisco penthouse. He'd handled the encounter badly and he couldn't get over the self-loathing he felt.

In a weak attempt to put her out of his mind, he had gone out on two dinner dates with women he would have previously been highly attracted to. Normally he would have enjoyed a couple of evenings of casual sex. Bu there was not one a spark. It was official. Molly had ruined him for any other woman.

Leilani had been correct – he had it bad.

His phone rang him out of his thoughts and as if she received a telepathic message two thousand miles away, Leilani greeted his gruff "hello".

"Have you gone to see her yet?"

With a big sigh, Carson threw his pen on the desk and sat back hard in his leather office chair. "Ya. I saw her."

"And?"

"And she doesn't want anything to do with me."

"I don't believe you. You didn't handle it right."

"You're probably right, but damnit, I showed up with my heart in my hands and she turned me away."

"Carson, what exactly did you say to her?"

"I asked her to have dinner with me while I was in town. She said it wasn't a good idea. End of story."

"That's it? You just asked her to dinner? You didn't tell her how you feel?" Carson could feel Leilani's eyes rolling through the phone.

"It didn't seem like good timing. I thought if I could just get her out to dinner with me, then I could tell her."

"You have to try again."

"I can't – she went to Italy."

"So?" Leilani was quickly losing patience with him.

"So, what? When she gets back I'll be in New York."

"No. I think you need a vacation. Someplace warm…say Italy."

Carson smiled into the phone as he looked down at the architectural plans laid out on his desk. They were almost complete.

"That would be amazing if she'd let me join her. But after last time, she'd probably personally drive me back to the airport to make sure I leave."

"You'll never know unless you try, now will you?"

"I suppose not."

"I gotta go. But you get yourself to Italy and sweep that woman off her damned feet!" Leilani slammed down the phone before he could object again.

A knock sounded at his office door, as his executive assistant, Meg, poked her head in. "I have your dry cleaning, Carson."

"Great, bring it in." He didn't bother to look up from the drawings before him until he noticed that Meg didn't leave his office.

She stood studying the suit that was just returned.

"Something wrong?"

"It looks like they weren't able to get that paint off the front of your suit. Do you want me to send it back or order a new suit?"

He felt a tingle along his spine when he remembered that last kiss with Molly. "No. Leave it. Thanks."

Silently, she left him alone.

Cursing his own weakness, he drew back from his desk and walked purposely toward the suit. He didn't touch it, but just looked at it for several long minutes. With a jaw clenched in determination, he waltzed to the door of his office and called, "Meg, I need you to book a flight for me…"

Molly stood in the museum looking at yet another "Madonna con Bambino" oil from yet another time period. She never tired of the different renditions of the traditional Mary with baby Jesus, but she did tire of seeing them alone after over a week. Perhaps that's why she accepted the invitation to dine from the handsome Italian waiter, Tonino. It was Sunday and his day off, so he was going to pick her up at the fountain in the square.

Molly was not interested in Tonino romantically, but he was charming and friendly and spoke a reasonable amount of English. She was desperate for some company and he wanted to take her to his favorite restaurant.

The quaint little restaurant only had a half dozen tables in it and soft Italian music serenading its customers. Tonino told her that his cousin owned the restaurant and that they would be served the chef's choice, which turned out to be one scrumptious course after another.

Tonino affectionately held Molly's hand when they sat dipping biscotti in frothy cappuccinos.

"Why you no have husband?" He kissed her hand, but she looked away.

"I – I don't know." She blushed at his direct gaze.

"You no find good man in America?"

As if all the air went out of her balloon, her shoulders drooped. "No. I found him, but he doesn't want me."

The shocked, indignant look on Tonino's face had Molly laughing. "Idiot!" He waved his hand as if to dismiss someone. "You love him?"

"Yes."

"You need good Italian man to make love to you. Make you forget idiot." He thumped his chest as if he knew just the person for the job.

"No, Tonino."

"You no like Tonino?"

"No – you're very nice, but I'm just not ready."

"He hurt you."

"Yes."

Gently, he took her hand in his and kissed first one side and then turned it over and tenderly kissed her palm. "If you change your mind, I am here."

"Thank you, Tonino. Dinner was lovely."

He drove her back to the cottage at breakneck speed, something she was getting used to about Italian drivers. When Tonino opened the door to her side of the car, she accepted his hand as she stood and then promptly fainted into his arms. He swooped her up with a gasp and awkwardly carried her into the small courtyard. From the shadows of the porch, Carson came forward, bolting off the bench on which he sat.

Tonino momentarily paused as he looked at Carson. Then he plopped Molly into Carson's outstretched arms and turned to go. When he came back with the purse that she had dropped, Carson spoke in a deep, angry voice.

"Did she drink too much?" Carson thought of the blue hawaiians that she'd had in Kauai and was surprised to here his answer.

"No vino." He raced out of there and jumped into his car. Carson had no choice but to search through Molly's purse for the key to the villa.

Successfully, he carried her into the bedroom and laid her gently on the bed. He retrieved a wet cloth and applied it to her forehead while he took in her appearance.

She had undergone some changes since he'd last seen her. Her hair had been cut so that there various layers which bounced in every which way, bringing out the natural curl that had been previously weighed down. It was also lighter in shade. Her makeup and clothing were more sophisticated, making her look older and more glamorous. She was stunning, he thought as she stirred.

Her eyes fluttered open and when she saw him leaning over her, they grew wide with surprise and wonder.

"Carson?" She thought she must be dreaming.

"Hello Molly," he said, his voice gruff.

"I'm dreaming," she yawned and rolled over onto her side away from him. As if realization struck her, she immediately sat up and swayed at the dizziness in her head. She laid back again.

"What did he give you, Molly?" Carson tried to keep the disapproval out of his voice.

"Who? What?" She rubbed her temple gingerly.

"That Italian guy. What did he give you to make you pass out?"

"I passed out? Oh. I fainted again." She smiled. It happened three other times since her trip to Italy and she was amused at the changes in her body.

"You don't seem very concerned about it," he was sitting on the side of the bed, wiping her temple again with the cold rag.

"I'm fine, Carson. What are you doing here? How did you find me?" Reality was sinking in and she was more confused than ever.

"I needed to see you, Molly. I have something to discuss with you."

Sensing his hesitance as he weighed whether or not now was a good time, she touched his hand with hers.

"I'm fine. What do you wish to discuss."

Without further prompting, he left the bed and returned a few seconds later with a long tube. He helped her to sit up against the pillows and the headboard, while he unrolled the diagrams and placed them in her lap.

"I don't understand," she was trying hard to review what appeared to be a floor plan, but it was all Greek to her. Why on Earth would he come all this way to show her his latest architectural design? She repeated. "I don't understand."

"Well, this one is the plot of land and the proposed landscape. This one is the master plan for the house, with the whole layout. And these are the different floors – two, plus a basement. What do you think?"

Her mouth had fallen open in dismay and she could only stare at him while she waited for him to explain further.

"It's our home, Molly. I bought some land in Marin about ten years ago. I haven't done anything with it yet, because I haven't had the motivation. But now I do."

He took her face in his hands and held her inches away from him.

"Marry me, Molly." His voice was gruff with emotion. "I'm crazy in love with you."

"But you don't believe in love," she whispered, her eyes moist from unshed tears.

He kissed her on the lips gently, and then with more passion before releasing her.

"I do now that I've found you. I had a tough childhood, Molly, but I want to believe. You make me want to believe. I once told you that the sexual woman was inside of you waiting to be released. Well, love has been inside of me waiting. I can't promise anything except that I'll try my damnedest to make you happy."

When she didn't say anything, but looked down at her hands, he took her face and drew it up to his.

"Say yes, Molly."

"Yes, Carson."

He kissed her again passionately and then tenderly.

"We'll get you the best doctors, Molly. I want you well and I want to spend a long, long life loving you."

He looked so concerned, so urgent.

"I'm ok, Carson, really." She touched her belly and then said pointedly, "We're ok."

"We?"

Slowly he realized just what she was saying. A lump crept into his throat as he gulped back a sob.

"Oh my God, Molly. You're pregnant? And you came all this way by yourself?" It exhilarated him – it scared the hell out of him - this idea of suddenly being a family. "How long have you known?"

"A few weeks." She smiled as he tried to comprehend it all.

"You didn't tell me when I saw you." It wasn't an accusation.

"I didn't want you to feel trapped. I was going to tell you eventually, but I was still getting used to the idea and was thinking about how I would raise him."

"Him?"

"Oh, I don't know – it's too soon to tell but my psychic tenant tells me I'm having a boy." She grinned.

"And you were prepared to raise him alone?"

She nodded. "I didn't want to, but I didn't want you to feel obligated."

He leaned his forehead against hers as he gathered himself. He wanted fiercely to protect her and the life growing inside of her. "You'll never be alone again – I promise."

He pulled her close and stroked her hair as her arms came up around his back.

"Carson, I want you," she pulled back enough so that she could kiss him with a passionate urgency that grew from weeks of being away from the man she loved.

"Are you sure it's ok?" He touched her tummy.

"It's better than ok – it's doctor prescribed! My hormones are out of control and you showed me what I'd been missing all these years."

Laughing, he pulled her into his arms and made sweet love to her in the little Italian villa.

Later, as she reviewed the plans, he chewed on his thumbnail, waiting for her reaction.

"We can change anything you want, Mol. It's just a place to start."

She grinned up at him and kissed him on the cheek. "I love it exactly the way it is, Carson. No worries."

Dear Reader,

Thank you very much for purchasing my book! I hope you loved my characters as much as I do!

If you enjoyed this love story, please take a moment to write a review on Amazon for me! It's very much appreciated!

Follow me on Facebook at **www.facebook.com/thewordflirt** for future updates and releases. Or visit my website at **www.wordflirt.com**. Until then – I hope you Believe in Love!

Sincerely,

Claudia Loens